MW01124594

REMO WENT WILD

Remo Cobb # 3

MIKE MCCRARY

BAD
WORDS INC.

To Knudsen who said, "Why'd you kill him? He's the best part."

WHERE WE LAST LEFT REMO & FRIENDS

REMO'S HEAD feels like the inside of a used diaper.

Forcing his lids open, he only finds more darkness before him. Hints and rumors of light peak out via slits and slants but only at the margins of his vision. More like the light is along the bottom and sides of something. Actually, it's exactly like light is working its way through the cracks of something that's over Remo's head.

"Hello?" he says.

"Hello," says Hollis.

"Hello," says Lester.

"Hello, gentlemen," Cormack says.

Remo trembles like a bomb went off inside his chest. An anger-shake shudders from the tips of his toes to the top of his cloaked head. He tries to get whatever's covering his head off but realizes his arms are bound behind him. His feet are strapped to the chair he's sitting in. He's guessing zip ties. It's embarrassing to admit he knows what they feel like, but he can't help but admire the quality of the material. Nothing but the best for the CIA.

"Can you take this fucking thing off my head?" Remo asks.

There's a long pause.

"Are you shitting me? You need me to say please?"

Another long, drawn out pause.

Without warning, the bag is ripped away, blasting blinding light into his face. With one eye open and one closed tight, Remo looks around, seeing that Lester and Hollis are also both zip-tied to chairs next to him. As he adjusts to the light, he can see they are in a small room in what looks like a modest home. Walls painted in accessible beige. Shit pictures on the walls and blackout curtains pulled closed on the windows. No telling if it's night or day, let alone what day it is. There's a high-intensity light shining on each of them like they were being interviewed on a TV show. Remo, Lester and Hollis can safely assume they are no longer in NYC based on the fact there is no street noise. There's no noise at all. There is a dead silence all around. No cars. No talking. Not even a damn cricket.

Cormack leans in the doorway dressed in his standard navy blue CIA garb. The expression on his face can be described as expressionless. He's neither happy, sad, nor angry. He is simply there. Shifting slightly to the left, Cormack now leans on the other side of the door. He clucks his tongue, raises his eyebrows, then holds his hands out as if looking for questions from his captive audience.

"Where would you like to start?" Cormack asks.

Remo, Hollis and Lester look to one another. *This guy, this fucking guy.*

"How about kick it off with *what the fuck, man?*" Remo says. "Or, *where the fuck are we?* Perhaps, *what was the fucking deal with those fucking darts* and, last but not least, *what in the fuck are you doing with us tied up like a trio of fucking fuckheads?*"

"Your buddy bashed Crow's skull in on the streets of New York."

"So?" Lester asks.

"Yeah, so what? It's done," Hollis says.

"We did the thing, we took out Crow," Remo says.

Cormack clucks his tongue again. He looks to the ceiling for some form of divine strength. "How are we supposed to question Crow now? Huh? He's barely alive in a hospital room and if he does pull through he'll more than likely only be able to urinate blood and meow answers."

"Sounds like a *you* problem," Hollis says.

Lester nods.

"Look. If you wanted this handled a certain way, Cormack, perhaps you should have been a little more specific with your instructions," Remo says.

"Now I know," Cormack replies. "I'll make sure this next one is explained in much, much more detail."

Silent pause in the room. Looks between Remo and his partners in crime fire off. Confusion circling the three of them.

"Next one?" Remo asks.

"Yes," Cormack says. "Meaning the one after the one you just did. Specific enough?"

"Wasn't the deal, man," Remo says, gritting his teeth.

"Did you think there was a deal? That's adorable. There is not. The only deal is you do what I want until I say we are done or you're dead. Does that provide the clarity you boys seek?" Cormack turns, leaving the room.

Remo feels himself deflating.

As if his bones and muscles have been nullified by Cormack, and he could simply spill out onto the floor into a puddle of goo. Any hope Remo had of being a normal person or a somewhat normal father to Sean is slipping through his fingers.

Perhaps gone.

Forever.

Cormack stops after a few steps then turns back to the room. "Okay. That wasn't completely fair, what I just did there a second ago. Sorry. Let me reset, okay? This next one, the one you boys are going to do, it's a big one. To be honest it's the one I really brought you in to accomplish, Remo. Oh, big thanks by the way for bringing in Lester. I hoped you would, but it really brings this thing together."

Lester stares.

The old Lester would gut Cormack right here and now without a hint of hesitation. Actually, the new Lester is considering it.

"You clowns left a hell of a mess to clean up in New York, but don't worry, I'll take care of it. It'll give Detective Harris something to do," Cormack says, then snaps his fingers as if he remembered something. "I've got some cash and prepaid credit cards for you, along with the clothes and weapons you'll need. You know, a good faith measure to show we're all one team." Cormack extends a hand, showing someone in. "My new friend will fill you in. I gotta bounce."

Cormack leaves.

As he clears the doorway, in walks a woman dressed in jeans and a torn man's dress shirt that hangs on her two sizes too large. She wears no shoes, nails firing off neon green.

It's the woman from the hotel.

The one who brought back Dutch's head.

The one who attacked Lester and Hollis in the alley.

The one who keeps dropping off fast-food napkins.

Hollis's and Lester's eyes bug out.

"Get that woman the hell away from me, man," Hollis says, trying to squirm away while still in a chair that's bolted to the floor.

Lester just stares at her with eyes wide as pies.

Remo looks to them, then to her. "Wait. I know you?"

She smiles sweetly, twisting her hair around her finger. "I'm Cloris." She waves to Lester like a schoolgirl with a massive crush. "Cloris Mashburn."

Remo and Hollis whip their heads around to Lester.

Lester looks like he's just been kicked in the balls. Twice.

"Mashburn?" Remo asks.

Cloris giggles, twisting her hair tighter. "As in Ferris, Chicken Wing and poor Dutch. Ya know? The head I delivered back to you. Those Mashburns. I'm the sister. Nice to meet you all." She looks to Lester. "You want to tell them what else, Buttercup?"

Remo's eyes slip to Hollis. *Buttercup?*

Lester shakes his head violently, like a toddler who doesn't want to admit he spilled grape juice on the new carpet.

Remo and Hollis are all ears, jaws on the floor.

"Lester and me, we're sweeties. As in engaged," she says, showing off her ring. "We're a bona fide thing."

BECAUSE OF HER VAGINA

Part I

CHAPTER ONE

CLORIS MASHBURN IS a train wreck of a woman.

Her face is a wadded-up ball of worry and rage as she peeks out over the rocky ridge. Something over there is troubling her deeply. Her stomach does flips while she sits looking down toward the base of a hill near Diablo Range, New Mexico. Her face flashes red. Teeth grind. Eyes laser-focused.

She can only watch as a house burns.

Her house.

Well, at least the house she shared with her three brothers and her lover.

There were a couple of other people who came in and out of the house, but it was always her, her brothers and the love of her life. The Mashburns were planning a series of robberies, so of course there were various goons and crime boys that came and went as the days passed. It was pretty common.

Cloris fell somewhere in the middle of the Mashburn family—wedged between Ferris and Chicken Wing, but younger than Dutch. Regardless of pecking order, they treated her like she was an infant. Always the little sister, no matter that she's older than

Chicken Wing (one year) and only slightly younger than Ferris (one year.)

She accepted that it was because of her vagina, but didn't like it.

She's a solid decade (or more) younger than her lover—well, fiancé—Lester. Lester became a part of the Mashburn crew about six months ago, or was it a year now? Cloris can't remember. What she can remember is how much she cares for that man. A big, strong, mean man who loves hard and doesn't mind going down on her. That's pretty much what Cloris had been looking for during her tumultuous twenty-five years on this earth.

Lester reminds her of her father. Ain't that the way? Aside from the going down on her bit. Let's not be gross. The way she sees it, most girls/women she's known have either been searching for their dads or for someone who will piss their dads off. Cloris had no intention of pissing off Daddy Mashburn.

That would be stupid.

Very stupid.

Daddy Mashburn, known as Big Daddy Mashburn in most criminal circles and to the law, isn't in the burning house, but Dutch, Ferris, Chicken Wing and Lester certainly are.

Cloris went on a walk to clear her head after a fight with Chicken Wing. Nothing serious. The usual. Chicken Wing was being a complete fucking dick to her and Lester. Lester took his bullshit in stride, but it upset Cloris. Strike that. It really pissed her off. She used to drag it out for days, would not let it go.

Lester took her aside one day, told her to just take a deep breath and walk away. Cloris found that odd, because she'd watched Lester beat the ever-loving shit out of more than a few people for talking shit. But she took what he said to heart and started following his words, not his actions.

This is why she's perched on this ridge, in the dirt, watching the house burn while the cops trade gunfire back and forth with her brothers and Lester. She should be in there blasting away, fighting alongside her people. She should be down there doing the thing.

She sucks in a deep breath. The head honcho cop calls out to his squad to stop firing. The pops and rat-a-tats of gunfire slow to a trickle, then a stop, with the last sound of a shotgun blast echoing, trailing off into the mountains.

The house still burns.

Flames lick the sky.

Everyone goes quiet.

Only the crackle of wood burning. The whisper of wind.

The door bursts open. Smoke spills out, twisting into the wind. The cops' tension ratchets up, their weapons ready, tracking on the door and what might come out. Every muscle in Cloris pulls wire-tight. She breathes in slowly and deeply, but exhales hard through her nose. Seconds pass like hours to her.

Dutch and Lester fall out through the smoke, landing in the dirt.

The cops rush in, jamming knees in their backs and planting hands on their heads, pushing their skulls into the ground.

Every molecule in Cloris is dying to run rip-shit down that ridge and do damage. Those fuckers shouldn't even think about touching them. She yearns to claw the eyes from those cops' fat skulls. Not so much for what they're doing to Dutch, more for them manhandling her man. Her Lester.

She bites her lip.

Her eyes pop.

Her face shakes.

"Get up slowly," a man says in a very cop-like voice.

The voice is behind her. She can't see the man's face, but she knows it's a cop. She's been around enough of them. A criminal with any kind of ear can tell just by the tone and the words chosen. Without allowing another second to pass she spins on the ball of one foot, letting lose a whip-strike with her other leg. Cuts the much larger man's legs out from under him. He drops down hard to the ground before he can even realize what's happened. As he lands with a thud his training kicks in.

He levels his weapon on her.

She kicks his gun hand away.

Cloris scampers with a quick grab, picks up a rock the size of a baseball and hurls a fastball strike to his face. His nose explodes. She grabs a bigger rock with both hands, kneels over him and slams the rock down like a prehistoric warrior.

The rock goes up then crashes down.

Over and over again.

Until she feels the fight is done.

"Not doing that," Cloris tells her father.

"Honey, Ferris and Chicken Wing, they're gone. Dutch and Lester are tagged, going inside as we speak." Daddy Mashburn stuffs cash and whatever else he can find into a trash bag. "Time to regroup, rebuild and rise up later down the road."

A ragtag group of criminals enter and leave the room, moving as fast as they can down the hall and in and out of rooms. Most of them covered in tats. Most of them armed. All of them carrying trash bags of money. They are in a safe house that's buzzing like a hornet's nest. The place is located in a town only a few miles from where the other house burned down to the ground. Daddy Mashburn has several of these places scattered around New Mexico. He's been working hard to put together a better situation, a more permanent, secure command center. A single compound for his operations. It is so damn close to being ready, but shit keeps getting interrupted.

"Only a matter of time before they find this place. Everyone's going to separate and we'll meet up at the new place."

"Is it ready?" Cloris asks.

"Real close. Damn close. The timing is actually not bad. Far from perfect, but the new place is going to rock and roll. Boost us into second level type shit." He pauses, pinches the bridge of his nose. "Kills me to lose the boys, it does, haven't had proper time to process the loss." He releases his fingers and stares deep into a crack in the wall, letting his mind unspool. He feels Cloris watching him. Snakes his head left and right, then says, "This is the life we signed up for."

He turns, facing Cloris. The look on his daughter's face freezes his heart. She's hurting. He knows it. She's pissed. He knows that too. He also knows his little girl, and his little girl will go full-on war machine at the flick of a switch. It's in her blood. Long family history of flick-switch war machines.

It's all in her eyes.

She's already gone.

That switch has done been flipped.

He takes her face into his thick hands, holding it like an egg. "Honey, Lester doesn't want you locked in some cage. He wants you to be free. He'd say the same if he was standing here."

Daddy Mashburn is a massive man. A physically imposing presence. Shoulders of a linebacker. He keeps his scalp free from hair, shaving it daily. His skin is also clean from tats. Thinks they are a silly game for the younger crop coming up now. Tagging themselves. Using them as ego-boosting signs of criminal allegiance or accomplishments. Making it easier for the cops to identify you. Young bucks using skin art to signal how many murders they've performed, like they were WWII fighter pilots marking their planes with the number of kills. He understands the need to put up a badass front. It keeps lesser fools at bay. But it also invites bigger badasses to take a swing and, oh yeah, makes the cops fully aware you've killed people.

Daddy Mashburn doesn't get it.

So damn silly.

His daughter feels differently. She'd tat up every centimeter of skin if she'd let herself. Use her body to scream out, release to the world what's been wanting to bust and spill out from her volcano mind. Unload what she feels. What she loves and what she hates. Her vanity keeps all that off her neck and face. There's a line for her and it stops at the collar of most shirts. Pretty much every other part of her is spoken for and covered in ink. She respects her dad's thoughts on the subject, which is why she always wears long-sleeved shirts around him.

Cloris looks into her daddy's eyes as her mind chews on what he said to her a few seconds ago. What he said about coming with him. She translates her father's words through her own filter. She hears it as him telling her to *play it safe. Do the smart thing. Give up. Stand down, little girl.*

She kisses him on the cheek.

Tells him softly, sweetly into his ear, "Fuck off, Daddy. I'm getting Lester back."

———

It's been a struggle.

Tracking down all the leads that lead nowhere. False info. Wrong turns. Glimmers of hope that flash and burn bright as the sun only to have them extinguished by the cold, hard realities of the truth. It's been a long, hard slog hunting and searching, day after day. Scraps of information keep her going. Burning love keeps her putting one foot in front of the other. Today, however, it's finally paying off. All the shit she's shifted through, all the doors she's kicked in, all the ass she's beaten down, and telling her big, scary father to fuck off has brought her here. Through it all she made it here. To this place.

They were here, she thinks.

All of them.

In the Hamptons.

She missed them by a few minutes, maybe seconds.

Here at the Hamptons home of one Remo Cobb there was a

fight. A big and bad one. Cloris tours what's left of the lawyer's place like she was a prospective buyer at an open house in a war zone. She's on the second floor inspecting the blown-out windows, the chunks of wall removed by bullets and shell casings scattered across the floor like confetti. Out the window she can see damaged trees and crude holes in the lawn churned up by gunfire.

Downstairs is where the real bloodbath must have taken place. The front door is a disaster. There's blood everywhere. Bodies dropped here and there. Most of them she doesn't recognize. Men who look like people she could have known. They look like the hard, rough crime boys who have surrounded Cloris her whole life, but she can't place any of these particular ones.

She stops.

There's one she does know.

Her brother Ferris is dead as Dillinger on the floor in front of her. She looks at the recent ice cream scoop-style wounds on his body. The gunshot wounds are past their prime, but they still produce an unmistakable level of nasty.

Her eyes moisten. She allows a single tear, but no more.

She follows a blood trail down the hall to a room. It's a study or an office of some kind, or at least it used to be. The door is busted all to hell. There's an overturned desk with large gashes removed by gun blasts. There's a blood-soaked knife on the floor. A half a thug laid out on the floor and another dead brother. Chicken Wing is stretched in a death spread, his upper body made up mainly of barely-held-together pulpy bits.

This time there are no tears.

A brief, shooting star of emotion that burned out before it started.

Barely a glance, then Cloris spits on Chicken Wing's lifeless face as she leaves the room.

Out in the back of the house is the strangest of sights. Yes, there is more blood and gunfire damage, but there's something new out here. Something strange. A headless body. Dutch's headless body, she's sure of it. She'd know his tats anywhere. This was her last brother. Much older brother. She doesn't offer up tears or spit for Dutch, because she never really knew him that well. Large age difference and all. She is somewhat curious as to where his head is, however.

The fact that Dutch, Ferris and Chicken Wing are here offers some clarity. They're dead, but they are here nonetheless, and it does confirm some ideas, while raising some new questions. The rumor was that Ferris and Chicken Wing survived the New Mexico shootout and were running with Dutch. Seems those rumors were true. Obviously the stories about Dutch busting out of prison are now confirmed to be accurate. Also a rumor about Lester being out as well. No signs of that, although the headless Dutch is possibly Lester's work. She's seen him do it in the past. Still, you can never be sure in this life.

There was also a rumor they were searching for their lost money. Which brings Cloris to some new questions.

Where does this lawyer, this Remo, fit in to all this? And, actually the only question that truly matters -- where is my Lester?

Her intense focus while searching the house has left her unaware of the sirens that have been screaming her way. Her moment of deep, questioning, analytical thought has left her in the incredibly vulnerable position of being alone in the middle of a crime scene. The lone living soul in a massacre.

Police cars skid in.

Doors fly open, then slam shut. Guns are drawn.

Cloris is told to get down on the ground.

She wishes she had a rock.

———

Cloris sits in a cramped cell.

Stinks of sweat and lost hope.

They've moved her twice. While she was staying in the first cell she beat the piss out of a drunk Hamptons millionaire who thought he'd have a grab at her tits. He'll be eating out of a tube for the foreseeable future. In the second cell she almost escaped by pulling off an almost impossible gymnast-style move up and over a guard who underestimated her abilities. Now, she's alone in a cell that's all hers to enjoy. A cell in the city so nice they named it twice. She's done New York many times, but not like this. Much different NYC experience behind bars and under lock and key. Her mouth is dry from screaming. Her face radiates heat from fighting back anger-tears.

She's been here for hours.

A little confused that she's not sitting at Rikers.

This place is different. She can't put her finger on it, but it is different.

She's not happy, but what the hell is she going to do about it? She chews a nail and lets the anger burn. Lets her imagination roll. Allows it to run down some dark corridors, thinking of all the possibilities of what's going on with her Lester.

Is he alive? Is he hurt? Is he fucking someone?

"Hello, Cloris."

She snaps loose from her thoughts. Looking up, she finds a man right out of central casting standing outside her cell.

Dark, navy blue suit.

Perfect government hair.

Hard government eyes.

CIA man Cormac smiles.

CHAPTER TWO

REMO AND HOLLIS ARE MOTIONLESS, like statues held hostage. They alternate their stares between Cloris and Lester while sitting zip-tied to chairs bolted to the floor. This woman just dropped one helluva bomb. Her announcement: that her and Lester were engaged.

Sorry, *a bona fide thing.*

This flies in the face of everything Remo and Hollis thought they knew about their new partner in crime. This isn't the Lester they know. The Lester they thought they knew. Lester, man of the Lord and violent avenger of whatever he feels like. That's their boy. Now what? He's a man with an emotional attachment? The pieces don't fit no matter how hard you try to jam them together.

"I'm sorry," says Remo, "you two are scheduled to be married?"

"Haven't set a date," Cloris chirps. "That shit takes time, ya know?"

Lester stares out into the void, wishing he were anywhere but here, hoping for a rescue that isn't coming.

"I have questions." Remo turns to Hollis. "You mind if I take the lead?"

Hollis shakes his head, unable to form his own questions.

"Shoot, counselor," Cloris says.

"One. Can you cut us free? Two... well, let's start with one."

Cloris cocks her head. "Later on one. Let's talk more, see how two goes."

"Okay. Two. How much do you know about your brothers?"

"A lot. They're dead. Found them at your house."

Remo sucks in a breath, glances to Hollis and Lester, then asks, "And Dutch?"

"I know you still have his head. It's in the other room, actually."

"Sorry, I should have been more clear. Do you know how it was removed?"

"Guessing someone in this room is responsible."

"And how do you feel about that?"

"Doesn't make me happy, but I'm willing to let it go."

Lester squirms.

"Big of you," Remo says.

"I think so. That all, counselor?"

"I have several questions about Cormac and you, but I'm assuming you two have a whole presentation of sorts on that."

"Something like that." Cloris smiles, giving her hair a twist. "I've got a question before I cut you boys loose. If that's okay?"

"Shoot," Remo says.

"Not for you." She turns to Lester. "Did you leave me, or did you just get caught up in all the stuff with my brothers and they wouldn't just let us live our lives together, even though you asked and pleaded repeatedly, but they were assholes not capable of understanding love, so consumed with their own bullshit that they told you 'no' so you felt trapped like a caged animal and didn't feel like you could come find me no matter how much you wanted to?"

Remo processes her question as fast as he can.

She gave him a lot there to work with.

She doesn't know everything. That much is clear. She doesn't know Lester split from her brothers. Doesn't know Lester never said a word about her, or the fact he's gone full-on saved by the Lord. She also doesn't know that Lester cut off Dutch's head. More importantly, Cormac didn't tell her everything.

Or...

Cormac did tell her everything and she's testing Lester right now, and if he gives the wrong answer she's going to cover all three of them in gasoline and light them on fire. She might feed them their own dicks first.

Remo's and Hollis's eyes slide over toward Lester. There's a lot riding on his answer and they're not exactly sure what the right answer is. They hope like holy hell he does.

Cloris looks to Lester with eyebrows raised, running her tongue over her teeth waiting for his response. It better be good. Damn good.

Lester clears his throat, pauses, then says, "Buttercup, I didn't know what to do. You know Dutch, he didn't want to hear a damn thing about me and you being together. Only had money on his mind."

Cloris's eyes soften, moisture forming in the corners.

"I tried. I did," Lester says.

Cloris wraps her arms around his neck, squeezing him tight.

Remo and Hollis exhale—thank God that worked. That was like watching a bomb being defused with the seconds ticking closer and closer to zero.

She weeps uncontrollably, trembling as she lets go of everything she's been holding onto these long, long days. Days and nights of crushing uncertainty. The searching. The hunting for her man and the truth. All the anxious churning in her stomach surrounding her and Lester. The not knowing what was true and what was bullshit. The rumors she's heard. The ugly rumors she never trusted.

That's all gone bye-bye. Removed by Lester's well-chosen words. Washed away by a tsunami of joy. Lester and Cloris are together and that's all that matters. They are back to being a bona-fucking-fide thing and the man she loves has told her everything she's been dying to hear.

Lester looks over to Remo and Hollis as Cloris sobs uncontrollably all over his shoulder. They give a thumbs-up, best they can at least with their hands bound, and plaster on over-the-top, massive smiles. *Way to go, bro.*

Lester mouths, *Help me.*

CHAPTER THREE

REMO TWISTS HIS FEET, first right then left, shakes his legs and squeezes his fists.

Working to get the feeling back into his wrists and hands after being bound by the tight-as-shit zip ties. His lower extremities are beginning to show signs of returning blood flow and his toes have stopped with their annoying throbbing. Lester and Hollis are up and free and rubbing the hell out of their wrists and ankles as well, just with less bitching than Remo.

Remo's head is still spinning from all that has happened in the last few days. It's a lot to take in, but there's no time to dwell on Russian roulette betting or the disaster in the streets of New York with Mr. Crow or the fact the CIA is fucking with him and his boys.

It's the CIA thing that's really eating at Remo.

Why them? Why the CIA? What's the international angle? Is there an international angle?

It has to be Remo's old clients. Maybe they have some global money-laundering ties or they funded some south-of-the-border cartel operations here and there. He'd heard that Crow dabbled in gunrunning for a blink of time, but he'd never heard anything vaguely global going on with the Mashburns. They are straight-up, good ole American crime boys. At least Remo thinks so. There's a gnawing, growing list of Cormac-related questions.

Why did Cormac go after Cloris?

Can anything Cormac said be trusted?

Doubtful.

Cormac said <u>this</u> is the one job he really wanted Remo for.

Why?

"Why?" Remo asks Cloris.

She's hanging all over Lester, trying to snuggle as close as she can with him. Lester is fighting her while trying hard not to show that he's fighting her. It's a delicate balance. Requires touch. Just like a teenager who doesn't know how to tell his girlfriend it's all over and he'd rather see other people. This situation is slightly more complicated of course, more life and death, but confused teenager is the look Lester's sporting at the moment and Cloris is completely oblivious to the vibe her dear sweet Lester is putting off.

Remo resets and tries again. "Cloris."

Nothing but more awkward hugs and shifts.

Lester taps her on the shoulder and points to Remo.

"What?" Cloris asks with a bit of bite.

"Why?" Remo asks.

"*Why* what?"

"Why us? Why now? Why you? Why does Cormac want us all together?"

"Oh." She plays with Lester's hair. "Daddy has a house not far from here. There's some other guys there too. Friends. Hired hands. Ya know, some sluggers, some battle boys. Cormac wants us to go in and kill 'em all."

"One more time?" Hollis chimes in.

"Simple. The four of us need to figure out a way to go into the house and kill everybody in there. More of a compound, really. Daddy's been working on the place for a while. *Kill 'em all.* Those were Cormac's words, not mine." Cloris takes in their blank stares. "We made a deal. Kill them. That was the deal. Simple shit really. Where did I lose you?"

Lester slips off to the side of Cloris, attempting to put a little space between them. "We're not a death squad."

Cloris giggles. "Since when?"

Lester opens his mouth to respond, but thinks better of it.

"Can we see the rest of the house?" Remo moves to the door. "Perhaps tell us where we are exactly? Last time I was conscious I was in an alley in New York."

Cloris takes Lester by the hand and bounces past Remo, leading the group into the living room. The décor is full-on mountain getaway cabin. Wood, wood and more wood. A fish on the wall and lots of bear art. Cloris escorts Lester to a plush-ish leather couch that's way past its prime. As they sink into the cushions Cloris wraps herself around Lester like a snake. Hollis and Remo look out the window. It's a gorgeous view of nature's glory. Trees and green in every direction with the bluest of skies peeking through. Mountains on the edges of their sight rest in the background. A running stream rolls not far from the front of the house. If they listen closely they can hear the water rumble and ramble. Remo isn't sure where this is, but it sure as shit ain't New York.

Remo points out the window, his face resembling a question mark.

"New Mexico. Pretty, right?" says Cloris.

On the floor in front of the fireplace is everything Cormac promised. Some rolls of cash, a small stack of prepaid credit cards, three separate piles of clothes and enough firepower to invade a tiny nation.

Remo and Hollis look over the spread. Lester tries to get up from the couch and join them, but is pulled back down by Cloris. She continues clawing at his hair. Can't take her eyes off of him.

The weapons are neatly laid out in sets of four. Four Glocks, four modified ARs and four pistol-grip assault shotguns. Boxes of shells, bullets and magazines are piled up with each set. There's also a convenient stack of Kevlar vests next to the clothing. Remo nudges his expert, Hollis, for an assessment of the weapons buffet.

"That'll do some damage," Hollis says. "Might be great. Might be shit. Depends on what we're walking into."

"Cloris, any idea when we are supposed to do all this killing you speak of?" Remo asks.

"Didn't get a specific time, but he did say *within a reasonable timeframe*." Cloris points toward the back of the house. "He's outside if you want to follow up."

Remo looks to Hollis then the back of the house. "He's fucking still here?"

"Yup," Cloris chirps.

Remo storms past the couch with Hollis close behind.

Cloris bounces up from the couch, dragging Lester by the hand toward a bedroom at the back of the house.

"Let's get the first one out of the way," Cloris says.

"Cloris..." Lester says.

"Don't worry. No worries if you blow one quick, I get it."

"No, I'm different now."

Cloris cocks her head.

"I changed in prison."

"You like dick now?"

"No."

"Can only do doggie? Had a friend who had a fella that got locked down in Huntsville and when he got out he could only do her doggie. Called her Bobby when he came. It'll be a transition, but I'm cool with it."

"No." Lester places his hands on the sides of her face. "I'm with the Lord now. I'm saved."

Cloris squints, scrunching up her nose.

"You know, God? That sort of thing," Lester says.

"That mean we can't fuck?"

"Yes."

"But you still kill people?"

"Yes, but only—"

"Is sex worse than violence?"

"Yes. No. Not necessarily. You're missing the—"

"Your rules are confusing, but this is how I see it. We're engaged, we should be married by now, which I think is enough gray area for us to go get weird for a few minutes."

She looks into his eyes, flicks her upper lip with her tongue and unbuttons the top two buttons of her shirt. Lester can't help but sneak a peek. It's been a while.

"How about this? No actual sex," Cloris purrs. "You use that magic tongue of yours and I'll take care of you too. Deal?"

Lester's breathing quickens.

Memories of the hot nights spent with Cloris bounce around his skull like a horny Ping-Pong ball.

His shoulders drop.

His will wilts.

She leads him by the hand into the room.

CHAPTER FOUR

REMO STORMS out of the house.

The cool, crisp mountain air hits his face and wraps around his body, giving him a refreshing blast of lovely. No matter how pissed he is, Remo can't help but love it. Actual fresh air can have a magical effect on a person. He didn't realize how much of a city boy he'd become over the years. Country-born and -bred, but the years of New York have changed him without a doubt. He hasn't felt the healing power of open, pure air in a long, long time.

It's nice, but there's no time to linger over this shit. He's heading straight toward a man who needs to answer a few of Remo's questions. Right the fuck now. He feels his anger fire up from his stomach to his face. Even the nice as hell mountain air can't cool off his rage.

Cormac sits on the hood of a white Chevy Yukon smoking a cigarette. This also pisses Remo off. This asshole is running Remo's life as if Remo were attached to strings and now, now this fucking dickhole is actually smoking in the mountains. Dicking up the nice, clean mountain air Remo was enjoying.

The balls on this guy.

"What special breed of a fucking fuckstick are you?" Remo asks.

Cormac blows a smoke ring up into the air.

Remo watches the ring break and dissolve into nothing. He takes a beat, resets and says, "You don't come off as a smoker."

"Watch porn too. We all got our stuff, Remo," Cormac says, then licks his fingers. "You seem unhappy. How can I make you happy?" Cormac holds Remo's eyes as he snuffs out the cigarette, crushing the tip by rubbing the lit end between his thumb and index finger.

The not so subtle symbolism isn't lost on Remo.

"So what? We're a bloodthirsty boy band now?" Remo asks.

"Look, if labels help you and your team, fine, but let's be clear on something. You started this thing. That's right, you. You set it all in motion the second you turned on the Mashburns. All of that —them, the money, prison, the little war in the Hamptons—that's on you and *that* has led us to here."

"Never once did I think this was what I was doing."

"Your intentions are irrelevant. Cute, but irrelevant. What is relevant is what's actually happening, and what's happening is you need to do something for me and your country."

Hollis steps up fast. Remo has no idea how long he's been there, but the look on his face has Remo thinking he's heard a lot. He looks Cormac in the eye and asks, "We waving flags now?"

"You're a former military man. Read all about you." Cormac smiles. "You're a bad man who's killed a lot of bad people. A lot of them not fans of the US."

"This ain't quite the same. Fairly sure you know that."

"Why? These people we're talking about, the ones hunkered down at Camp Mashburn, are indeed enemies of this country. And"—Cormac stabs a finger into Remo's chest—"this is an excellent chance to finish them off. Put a cherry on top of the fine work you started."

Remo's mouth goes dry.

All the memories of the Mashburns flood his brain like a dam busting wide open.

Their vicious nature. Their insanity.

All the blood. The pain. The fear.

From behind Remo a loud spank echoes, followed by a quick, sharp yelp.

Remo and Hollis look back to the house then return to Cormac.

"What about Cloris?" Remo asks. "She get to be the surviving Mashburn in all this?"

Cormac clucks his tongue and looks to the house. "That, sir, is up to you. She's here to help you without getting you killed. Think of her as a key to the front door. She's the only link to them and the best way inside."

"You can't just send in your own squad of CIA murder boys? You got plenty," Hollis says.

"We do. You're right. But we'd have to go in with force. Gun blazing kind of deal and we'd win, eventually. We did that very thing here in the mountains not that long ago." Cormac looks to Remo. "You remember, right? That's when we got Dutch and your pal, Lester. Thought we killed Ferris and Chicken Wing. We were wrong, but you two took care of that later in the Hamptons. Didn't you?"

Remo nods.

Hollis nods.

Cormac gives them a finger gun with a wink. "Good work, boys. The problem was that during our little firefight here in New Mexico we lost a lot of good people. And by *we* I mean law enforcement. CIA was nowhere near that mess. So the burning question is why put good women and men in danger when I've got you."

Remo studies Cormac. He's become really good at reading people over the years. The problem here is Cormac is a master at giving up nothing. Cormac has had the jump on Remo since the day they met. Remo couldn't find a crack in his bullshit. A first for Remo, but now he has a read on something. He senses something is locked up behind those eyes of Cormac. He just needs to wiggle it free.

"You don't know where they are," Remo asks, "do you? I mean you know they are in this state, but you have no idea where or how many of them there are. Am I right, buddy?"

Cormac smiles, impressed with Remo. He's rarely surprised, but Remo has made a career out of surprising a lot of people. Remo keeps unspooling his thoughts while trying to read Cormac's eyes.

"Cloris didn't tell you everything, or rather, not much of anything," Remo says. "She traded up to get to Lester and now it's time for her to pay up by getting us into the Mashburn compound."

Cormac shrugs without confirming or denying anything. He motions for Remo to come over to him. With great reluctance Remo moves toward the Yukon, standing in front of Cormac.

"Remo, man," Cormac says low so only they can hear, "I know you don't have any reason to trust me."

"Nope."

"No reason to believe anything I tell you."

"You're right, and I do not."

"Do you really have a choice though?"

Remo stares back at him, burning. His insides on fire because Cormac is right and not having a choice is not a place Remo likes to hang out. Hollis, not liking the vibe, begins to move their way. Remo holds out a hand, requesting a moment. Hollis stands down.

"Trust me or not, I'm being straight with you here," Cormac continues. "After all this Mashburn unpleasantness is over with you will be free and clear. Can't promise that you'll ever get your life back. You probably won't. Certainly never be the same. I can't promise your kid will love you forever either, but what I can promise you is a chance for you to find out."

Remo looks anywhere but Cormac's eyes. Trying to find a clear thought.

"You do this thing and you're good with me. No strings. All done," Cormac says, holding out a hand. "Cool?"

Remo eyes the extended hand that's hanging, waiting for a confirmation shake. He's made a lot of deals with the devil. At times, he's been the devil. He takes a moment to try and read Cormac one more time. Straining to use all his powers, his gifts, all the ability he's developed over the years to break down the human race into simple, digestible pieces. Even with all of that, Remo is still not sure with Cormac. This CIA man is good. Real good. He's also right. Remo has no choice but to trust him.

Remo shakes his hand.

"Good," Cormac says, then holds up a finger like he forgot something. He raises his finger up into the air and swirls it three times.

From the trees, from out of nowhere, four men appear.

Remo jump-bounces back. He'd almost screamed but he stopped himself.

Hollis simply sets his feet and balls up his fists.

The four men are in full-on tactical gear. Dressed in black. Helmets, vests, guns strapped on and hard, lifeless eyes that dig into your soul. They surround Cormac as he slides off the hood of the Yukon.

"I recognize there's a chance the Mashburn place might have anywhere between two and two hundred armed, mean and nasty people inside. As you stated correctly before, I really don't know. Not sure Cloris does either." Cormac motions around him. "This, these people here, this is your backup. Your nuclear option. If things get too hot you call them in, but not until you get inside and have eyes on the man affectionately known as Big Daddy Mashburn."

"And how do we contact these pretty little kill boys? Do I do that cute finger swirl thing?" Remo rubs his face as the uncomfortable rush that comes from a sudden spike in blood pressure takes hold of him.

"We'll get you set up with communications," Cormac says.

Hollis stares. Blinks. Rolls his eyes.

Remo wants to throw up.

"What could go wrong?" Cormac says with a cluck of his tongue.

Cloris and Lester exit the house in a post-orgasm stumble. Both of sport head of hair that resemble bird's nests. Lipstick smeared across Lester's blank face. Massive, toothy smiles on hers.

"S'up, fellas?" Cloris asks.

CHAPTER FIVE

"WHAT IN THE name of good fuck is the plan?" Remo asks.

He receives little in response. Maybe a glance, a flash of eyes, but certainly nothing that would be considered a response. The four of them are now back in the living room staring at the buffet of weapons and clothes laid out on the floor. Hollis begins inspecting the guns one by one. Cloris holds onto Lester tight. Lester stares out into the void. Lost as hell. He enjoyed the pleasure bounce earlier, but the glow has faded back to the realities of the situation.

Remo slips off from the group and heads back outside. The porch creaks and moans as he steps across wood that has been battered by the elements over the years. He takes a seat in an old rocking chair that offers one helluva view.

He uses that view to help his head spill out the events of the day. Watching the wilderness before him helps soothe the shittiness in a way. Makes it all seem not so bad. Remo knows he's fucked, but a nice view coupled with a nice breeze can fool the shit out of you if you'll just let it.

Before Cormac left he gave Remo a device he can use to *communicate* with the CIA murder goons/kill squad/nuclear option.

It's a small, tiny-ass thing that he could crack between his fingers. There's a small pull-strip adhesive so it'll stick to something. Cormac recommended somewhere safe, like on his person or on the side or underneath of an object that won't see much action. Once the device breaks, it will send a signal to the kill squad they can zero in on, and they will come riding in with guns blazing. He was told they will not respond unless Remo is inside and they have *reasonable confidence* Remo has *viable intelligence*.

Remo made a joke about his LSAT scores.

Get it? Viable intelligence? LSAT?

The joke didn't land with Cormac. Or the kill squad.

Humorless fucks.

Once they are inside the Mashburn place and they know the layout and an approximate number of bad guys and have put eyes on Big Daddy Mashburn, then Remo is to break the device and say the words *burn it down.*

Remo asked if he could spice it up with "Burn this motherfucker down" or "Let's light this bitch the fuck up." He received blank stares, a couple of blinks and a snort in return, then was told they will only respond to the agreed upon verbiage.

No vision among these people.

Fuckers.

Burn it down is just a little dramatic, he thought, perhaps a touch macho, but he was in no position to question what his personal CIA attack team wanted to use as a safety phrase. If *burn it down* gets them to their happy place, then so be it.

Remo's got bigger issues at the moment.

Management issues.

The management issue facing Remo right now is how the hell he's going to bring together the shit show that is currently his team. A team he never asked for. A team he did not recruit. A team of people that has killed more people than french fries. These people are not only his team now. It's more serious than that—this group of whackos will have a lot to do with Remo's survival. Meaning, they will also play a huge part in helping Remo get out of this mess. Remo still holds onto hope that Cormac will make good on his promise of getting Remo free and clear once this is all over. Getting Remo back to some form of a normal life.

A life with his son. Just a good, normal life.

There's still hope.

You lose hope, you lose everything.

Remo is still a realist, however. He knows that *normal* has been lit on fire and thrown out a window, but he does hope he can find some way to become a functioning member of society. It won't be conventional, to be damn sure, but Remo knows he can work it out. Find a way to make it all come together. That's what he does.

He figures shit the fuck out.

He only needs Cormac to do what he says he's going to do. Unfortunately it's a major piece of the puzzle, and not one Remo can control or really count on. Cormac kinda said the same shit before that last little thing with Mr. Crow, yet somehow, after Remo took care of Crow—well, Lester and Hollis played a role— but after that Crow thing was resolved Remo ended up tied to a chair with a bag over his head in New Mexico.

Trust in Cormac is some thin crust-style shit, at best.

Unfortunately, trust and hope in hopelessly untrustworthy people is territory Remo is all too familiar with.

And Remo is back where he was before he came outside.

Completely fucked with limited, shit options.

Hollis takes a seat in an old, busted-up rocking chair next to Remo. He says nothing, looking out over the trees watching the branches sway slightly, the peacefulness of the place taking him by the hand. Hollis closes his eyes, lets the moment breathe, forgets all the shit the man next to him has put him through. Sets aside all the shit this man is going to put him through in the future. The very near future. He should snap Remo's neck, kill the other two inside, take the money on the living room floor and take off to find his wife and kids. Wherever they are. Hollis smiles. He maps out the whole thing in his mind, playing a movie only he can see. A movie where he's free of these people and living happily ever after with his family. A life he should be enjoying right now. A life interrupted by Remo.

"What you think?" Remo asks.

"Shut the fuck up before I snap your neck, is what I think."

Remo nods then closes his eyes as well.

They'll talk later.

CHAPTER SIX

CLORIS SERVES UP A LARGE, steaming plate of chicken pepperoni. She smiles at Lester as she places the plate in the center of table, carefully placing the serving spoon and fork on either side.

It's Lester's favorite.

Cloris knows it.

Lester knows it.

"What is it?" asks Remo.

"Chicken pepperoni," Cloris says, setting down the Caesar salad. "It's Italian-ish. Dig in and chill out."

The plate looks magnificent. A mouthwatering, bubbling red sauce covering a pile of perfectly breaded chicken breasts with mozzarella and thick slices of pepperoni spilling out from the sides, and it's all sitting upon a mountain of cloud-like pasta.

Lester watches her serve his friends like a perfect little hostess. He's not sure he's met this woman before. She plates Remo first, then Hollis, letting Lester watch. Letting the sight and smells of his favorite meal wash over him. Cloris knows this guy and she knows a little sexual release and a good meal will bust him wide open.

Confusion streams, swirls inside Lester's brain. He wants to jump up from the table, run screaming into the mountains and never come back. He wants nothing more than to leave this woman, this house, this situation as fast as he can, but he knows damn well he cannot.

That fact sticks in his brain like a pitchfork.

In a way, he's already tried.

Sort of already tried to leave.

It's not like he was trying to work a fake death or anything. He just used the shootout and jail as a convenient way of getting out from under a relationship he felt should have ended a while back. It happens all the time. Not like this, of course, but relationships do end. People break up. No big deal. Lester's situation was complicated by the fact she's the boss's daughter and, oh yeah, the boss is a crime boss and, oh yeah, the daughter has a bit of a temper and carries a prominent violent streak.

"This is pretty fucking good," Remo says with mouth stuffed, red sauce dripped on his chin and pasta snaking up to his lips.

"Thank you, Remo," she says.

"And she cooks too," Hollis says with a *complete prick* grin to Lester.

Hollis cuts a big bite of chicken with just the right amount of cheese and pepperoni and swirls a healthy amount of spaghetti onto his fork. He snickers to himself, taking some pride in his little dig at Lester—it's fun for Hollis to fuck with Lester. Then he notices the death stare firing off from across the table.

Cloris grips her knife with eyes locked in on Hollis. It's as if the temperature in the room dropped thirty degrees. Her stare bores into Hollis.

Hollis chews slowly, assessing the situation. He holds his knife as well.

Remo and Lester both take note of this potential problem.

"He didn't mean anything," Lester says. "He was making a joke. Busting balls."

"That it?" Cloris asks Hollis. "You being funny?"

Hollis swallows. He'd rather not get into a thing with her. He's fought women before, really tough women that almost killed him, and he's pretty sure Cloris falls into that category, but he also doesn't want to back down and let Cloris think she's running this thing, or running him for that matter.

"Just having a little fun with Lester, that's all. We've been through a lot together. That okay by you?"

"You think a woman's place is in the kitchen?" Cloris asks. "That the kinda joke you're making, funny man?"

Remo wipes his mouth, not liking the mood of the table. "Okay, okay, people. It's been a rough few days for everybody. Let's press reset and enjoy this great dinner Cloris put together."

"No, I don't think a woman's place is in the kitchen. My wife was an attorney before she decided to give up her practice and stay home with the kids. I think a woman's place is wherever she wants to be. Same as a man. If a woman wants to be a CEO, a housewife or give handjobs for crack in Central Park that's her call and nobody, regardless of genitalia, should tell her otherwise. That make sense or should I talk slower for you?" Hollis says.

"Can we just enjoy the fucking chicken?" Remo asks.

Cloris slices the air with knife toward Remo. "Suck it, counselor." She points the knife back to Hollis. "Since you're so fuckin' in tune with the vagina movement, what's the joke? What's so goddamn funny about me making dinner?"

Lester's and Remo's eyebrows rise without allowing eye contact to happen. Both hoping the conversation will simply run out of gas on its own.

"Look, if you're going to jam me into an answer, I'll oblige," Hollis says, pointing his knife to Lester then back to her. "The joke I was making with Lester was based on the fact he's been a little, I don't know, off since you showed up. That's really it, Cloris. Has jack shit to do with your kitchen wizardry or what's between your legs."

Cloris leans back, stabs a pepperoni with her knife and gnaws at it while thinking over what Hollis just said. The gears behind her eyes crank as her teeth gnash. She simply does not like this guy.

Something in Hollis has clicked. Somewhere in his head he's made the transition from just wanting to get along to wanting to push some buttons and see where this goes. See where she'll go. Hollis needs to know who he's about to go to war with.

"Looking back now, your little drop-ins in New York," Hollis continues, "you dropping fast-food napkins. You knew what the hell was going on."

Lester swallows then says, "I suspected it."

"First time we fucked was in a burger joint bathroom," Cloris says. "It was dirty-sexy-brilliant."

"Buttercup," Lester says. "Not helpful."

"It was magic," she says. "Eat."

"Perhaps you should have made burgers then," Hollis says.

Cloris cocks her head, eyes again boring into Hollis.

Lester and Remo look down. Eyes only at their plates, while shoveling in food as fast as they can. As if the secret code to getting the hell out of this meal is written at the bottom of the plate.

The silence is deafening.

Forks scrape plates. Chewing. Stares hold, break, then fire off again.

The room is an ever-expanding balloon of tension with everyone sitting on edge watching, waiting for it to explode.

Cloris tears off some bread, chews, sits watching Hollis.

She's boiling inside.

Hollis glances up to her, smiles, then looks back down to his plate. He cuts another big bite and says, "I don't know about the bathroom sex, but I must say, the chicken is fantastic."

Cloris launches herself up and over the table.

Hollis catches her in mid-air and the force sends them falling back in his chair. They slam to the hardwood floor. The chair cracks in two. There's a dull thud of meat hitting wood. A crunch of bone. Plates fly. Glasses dump. Salad goes airborne.

Cloris and Hollis roll over and over. A tumbleweed of violence. Muscles tight. Veins pop. Faces red. Each holds the other's knife at bay. Spit flies from Cloris's mouth as she screams, barking in tongues. Hollis is fighting to play defense, but Cloris's anger is fueling a level of attack strength he wasn't expecting.

Lester and Remo throw their chairs back from the table, but neither has any idea what to do or how to stop this. They pivot on the balls of their feet, dancing a dance of uncertain steps. Both think of jumping in, but stop as Cloris's and Hollis's knife blades slash back and forth. Remo and Lester end up simply standing there with faces slack, jaws dropped.

"People," Remo says without a clue. "What the fuck?"

Lester eyes the floor. He picks up a piece of chicken by the broken chair and starts chomping it down. It helps him think.

Cloris and Hollis fire straight up, springing to their feet. Squaring off like gladiators. Hollis grabs a chair using it to hold off Cloris as she swipes and stabs her steak knife wildly. Hollis the lion tamer works the chair, sticking and jabbing the legs at Cloris. Sweat drips as he attempts to back her into a corner of the room. He's working it slow as he can, an inch at a time, backing her up a little here and a little there. So subtle she doesn't notice what's happening.

Remo follows them with Lester behind him, still taking down the chicken.

"Cloris," Remo barks, "let's take a breath and figure this the hell out. We need each other, remember?"

Cloris glances to Remo, kicks at Hollis. "Then tell your boy to stand the fuck down."

"Hollis?" asks Remo.

"Tell her to stop trying to gut me and I'll consider it."

"Can't promise that," Cloris says.

Cloris sees a flash of a moment. A wrinkle of an opening.

Hollis has let his focus slip to Remo for just a blink, but long enough for her. She kicks the chair hard to left and pounces like an animal. She slams into Hollis like a hard-hitting battle ram, sending them both smashing back down to the floor. Both lose hold of their knives upon impact sending them sliding across the floor. Wailing like a child torn from the wild, she grips Hollis by the ears, slamming his head down on the wood floor.

Hollis's sight flashes white, but he pulls himself back in. He fires a leg straight up, almost getting it up over her face and down her body. She wiggles left and right like a world-class cage fighter, avoiding getting caught in his vice leg grip. She rips a lighting punch. He whips his head right, clear from the strike. Her fist cracks into the wood. Her bones crunch. Biting down on her lip she sticks a fist to his nose with other hand.

Remo can't believe his eyes.

Hollis is losing.

She tags him again in the face.

From the corner of her vision she spies one of the knives. Its slide was stopped by Lester's suitcase against the wall. Diving free from Hollis, she grabs the knife and spins back around, landing on her knees. Cloris grips the knife with both hands, raising it high up over her head, about to jam it down into Hollis's chest.

A thick slab of chicken pepperoni slaps her in the face.

Lester dive-tackles her away from Hollis pinning her down on the floor.

"Breathe," Lester tells her with his large hands holding her down. "You need to breathe and chill, Cloris."

She fights it.

"Do it." He presses. His face hard but calm.

Cloris sucks in and out through her teeth. Her skin is bright red. A single stream of blood snakes down her cheek. Lester can see her pulse bump inside the veins of her neck. Her eyes are locked onto his. Like a semi-crazy Lamaze coach, Lester is actually bringing her down to a normal level by his presence and the sound of his voice.

"Breathe."

She obeys.

Remo helps Hollis up to his feet. Hollis will never admit it, but Remo can see the man is shaken. A warrior like Hollis can't afford to admit when he's been beaten. Challenged, sure, but never acknowledge a defeat. That's the kind of thing that can dig into the skull of a man like Hollis. He needs to believe he can walk into anything and kill everyone. Hollis knows it. Remo knows it. Remo also knows he needs his boy's shit wire tight. He needs Hollis firing on all confidence cylinders. He needs his killing machine humming. A good leader knows exactly what to say to his or her people at moments like this.

"She fucked you up, man," Remo says.

Remo is a horrific leader.

Hollis simply glances his way, then kicks him in the balls.

Remo folds like a dish towel then drops to the floor. First to his knees and then full-on fetal.

Hollis quietly seethes. He sees Lester's roller suitcase from New York against the wall. He steps over Remo and rushes over to it. Hollis unzips the top and pulls out Dutch's severed head by the hair. He holds it up for all to see.

"See this? This is what your sweetie did to your brother," Hollis yells.

He turns slightly and punts the head like a football. Dutch's head sails awkwardly across the room, crashing through the window. Glass falls, bouncing off the wood floor like a spilled bag of jelly beans.

Remo watches through his broken-ball tears.

Lester shakes his head.

"Fine! He was a fuckin' asshole anyway!" Cloris screams, then she sweetly turns to Lester. "I forgive you. You did what you had to do, I'm sure of it."

Hollis rolls his eyes.

Lester can only stare at her, taking in the crazy as he has her pinned on the floor, the slab of chicken pepperoni still plastered to the side of her face.

Remo grunts, holding his nuts.

Tomorrow they're going to storm Camp Mashburn.

Go team.

CHAPTER SEVEN

REMO SITS beside his son Sean in front of a crackling campfire. Roasting marshmallows, telling ghost stories and loving it. The smiles are big. The night sky is deep and dark. The laughs are huge. This is what Remo wanted for his life. This is what Remo hoped he'd get when he double-crossed the Mashburns in the first place. He didn't know it at the time, but this is what he was doing. This was the goal. His brain was taking him to this, even if he didn't realize it at the time. His body and soul were working to get to this place without his day-to-day lizard brain putting it all together for him.

Perhaps there could have been easier ways to get here.

Perhaps if Remo was in his right mind, sans the booze and drugs, he would have come up with a stronger plan than pissing off homicidal maniacs, but he didn't and here we are.

Remo has never done things in a straight line.

Never the easy path.

What's the fun in that?

"Thanks, Daddy," says Sean. He gives a smile that melts Remo's heart upon impact.

Remo feels his eyes swell, water building up, about to bust

open floodgates. He puts an arm around his boy and holds on tight. These are the moments that make it okay. That make the shittiness of the world and people in it bearable.

"Time to go," Anna says.

Remo's heart freezes.

He turns around to find his ex-wife walking out from the thick, dark forest behind them. She's wearing the dress she wore on their wedding day. White. Flowing. Gorgeous as she ever was, but her face is twisted and wracked with emotion. She's here to do something she doesn't want to do, but has to. A mother who knows that parenting isn't always smiles and giggles. She's here with a job to do.

"I'm sorry," she says, "but Sean needs to leave."

"What? Why?" Remo asks, stumbling as he stands up. "We're just getting started."

Anna shrugs her shoulders.

"Sorry, Daddy," Sean says. "Should have fucking started sooner, prick."

Sean punches Remo in the gut then takes his mother's hand, storming off into the woods.

Remo holds his stomach, mouth wide in complete shock.

There's a rumbling sound behind him. Something primal.

Remo whips back around. There's a wave, a mass of movement coming at him. Charging. Their speed is relentless. Hundreds of them. An army of headless men running at him holding crude weapons made of bone and rock. All covered, caked in dirt and blood.

Remo closes his eyes.

Accepts his fate.

CHAPTER EIGHT

REMO JOLTS AWAKE.

He finds himself laid out on the couch with the chilly night mountain air whistling through the busted-out window. Releasing a huge sigh, Remo sees his breath exit his lungs, circling and twirling into the air, creating a spirit-like shape above him. His brain starts to unwind, watching his spirit-breath dissipate into nothingness. That dream he just shook loose from twists inside his head like a fat worm working its way around his very thoughts. He shakes his head hard, as if his brain were an Etch A Sketch. His thoughts shift to tomorrow, or today; he has no idea what time it is, or the date for that matter.

What the hell is he going to do?

Can Cloris deliver? Can she get them into Camp Mashburn?

Are they walking into certain death?

Will Cormac fuck him over no matter what happens?

Should he jump and run right now, take his chances and hope like hell that Sean and Anna will take him in?

"We're in trouble," Lester says.

Remo jumps-bounces up into a seated position and yelps, "What the fuck, man?"

Lester shushes him, pointing to the back rooms.

"What the fuck, man?" Remo whisper-barks.

"She's crazy."

"No shit."

"She'll kill us all."

"So you're saying you don't trust her."

"I trust her to be her."

"What the hell does that even mean?"

"If she wants something, she cannot be stopped, but what she wants can change dramatically with little or no notice or reason."

Remo thinks on that one. His mind gnaws it, chews away at it. He's dealt with many members of the criminal element, most of them less than sane, and he has known a few people who fit exactly what Lester has just described. One thing is certain: things rarely end well with that sort of folk.

"Well, what should we do, Lester? I'm asking because I really don't know. We don't have a strong play here. Not much in the way of a choice that I can see. Cormac more than likely has people watching us right now. If we don't go after the Mashburn place, we're fucked. Fucked hard. Not the beautiful, 'sweet act of love' kind of fucked."

Now Lester chews on that one.

Remo watches him sitting in the darkness. He's never seen Lester like this. Conflicted. Unsure. Off-kilter and all bunched up over another human being. Lester has come to Remo in several forms. Hard-as-hell criminal. A killer. A savior. A friend, of sorts. But never as a man busted up by a woman.

"If you want to run, I get it," Remo says. "I've had some women that have made me want to cut and run. There's probably more than one woman who would say the same about me. Of course, never had one who could take down a highly functional hit man, but that shit's neither here nor there."

Lester looks to the ceiling and closes his eyes. Remo sees him begin to mumble to himself in the moonlight.

"What's that, friend?" Remo asks.

Lester continues his chat with himself.

Remo snaps his fingers at him, trying to get his attention.

Lester opens one eye, looking in his direction, then shuts it immediately, going back to his conversation.

Remo is getting pissed here. It's a little rude, this thing Lester's doing. He can feel his anxiety rising until he realizes something.

The man is praying.

"Oh. I'll shut the fuck up. Sorry, man," Remo says.

Remo tries not to stare, but he really doesn't know what to do with this. It's quiet in the house, save for the slight whisper coming from Lester's chat with the Lord and the wind kicking up through the shattered window caused by the Dutch head-punt earlier. Remo has nothing to do. It's making him uncomfortable. As if he's a third wheel. He folds then unfolds his hands. He looks around the room three, four times. Finally he lies down, staring at the ceiling. For a moment he considers praying himself. It's been a while.

A long while.

He was raised in Texas, and church was a big thing in his neighborhood, even though most of the people he knew growing up weren't exactly strict followers of the Bible. Not outside the walls of church at least. They sang the songs and recited the words they were told to recite, but once they left the building they went back to doing whatever the fuck they wanted. Mainly being self-serving assholes.

His father was a perfect example.

The man drank and fucked everything he could. He beat his kid and gambled like a son of a bitch. But, by God, he was at church every Sunday morning singing his balls off. Maybe it was his only redeeming quality. Maybe the old man was just hedging his bets on the whole heaven gamble. The big dice roll in the sky. Remo has his guesses, but he'll never really know. The old man didn't discuss much of anything when it came to his philosophy on life, let alone his thoughts on the afterlife. Lester seems to have a better a handle on the religion side of the equation. Maybe the man and/or woman upstairs can provide some light on the situation they're in. Perhaps a conversation with the Lord will allow Lester to loosen up his thoughts and allow him to come up with something that will help them.

Can't fucking hurt, thinks Remo.

"I have an idea," Lester says.

Remo sits up, all ears. The Lord did give him something.

"We need to kill her," Lester says. "You know, before she does us."

Remo blinks, then lies back down.

CHAPTER NINE

No one says a word at breakfast.

Only the sound of forks scraping plates. The occasional cough.

Little eye contact.

Lester says grace.

Cloris sits stone-faced, burning a spot on the table with her stare.

Remo thinks he should have run, but enjoys the food.

Hollis made eggs and bacon.

CHAPTER TEN

EVERYONE SITS in silence in the living room.

Except for the brief conversation between Lester and Remo, and then Lester and the Lord, literally no one has said a word since the Chicken Pepperoni Incident. Inside, Remo is burning. He can't take it. He knows what's at stake and he can't let this stubborn pride, whateverthefuck wall of immeasurable bullshit, stand in the way of him getting clear with Cormac. Even if Cormac is completely full of shit and will never let him go.

Hope.

Hope is all he's got.

All that's left.

It's not great, can't sink your teeth into it, it's not what Remo wants, but it's where he is in his life. Hope that a son of a bitch CIA man will deliver on what he said he'd do.

Remo thinks he had stronger odds playing Russian roulette at Crow's.

Remo remembers something Chicken Wing told him once. Something Chicken Wing's older brother Dutch told him. He said, "We are the sum of our mistakes." At this particular moment Remo can't argue with that statement or the mathematics of it.

The math on Remo has brought him to this place, without question. Here, now, in this room with these people at this moment in time.

Not much sense in fighting it, Remo decides.

Gotta roll with it, baby.

Remo clears his throat. "Okay. I'm not going to rehash what happened. I hope we can agree that shit was unfortunate, right?"

He looks around the room. He gets nothing verbal in the way of confirmation. Only tops of heads bobbing. Slightly. He'll take it.

"Look, we have to work together. Don't have a choice. None. The CIA doesn't give a single damn about our conflicts. They want us to go after the Mashburn place. Period. I don't like it. I don't want to do it. But it's what we've been tasked with, and dammit, if this is what we've got to do to get free then, dearest motherfuckers, that's what we're gonna do."

Heads pick up a bit.

Remo stands and continues. "Not the time for bullshit. Now, I have no idea what is waiting for us out there at this Camp Mashburn. I don't." Remo's feeling it now as he moves around the room. "We could be stepping face-first into a sausage grinder. But what I do know is that we are tough people. A real squad of badass individuals. Badasses capable of some badass shit, and together we can rain down some serious damn damage."

All eyes on Remo now.

"Most of us in this room have killed some of those piece of shit Mashburns." Remo pauses. "Sorry, Cloris."

Cloris shrugs. *No problema*.

Hollis grins.

Lester nods like he's gobbling up Remo's sermon with a fork.

"We've got tools on the floor and work to be done. Hard work, no question, but I have no doubt in my mind that we can put our bullshit in the rearview and end these motherfuckers. Am I right?"

Nods from his people.

"We got this?"

Hollis stands.

Lester follows.

They all look to Cloris. The only one left seated. She crunches some bacon she brought in from the kitchen.

"I've gone to war with these guys. I trust them with my life," Remo says, speaking directly to Cloris. "I'm going to extend that trust to you. Will you help us do this thing?"

Cloris's eyes slip over to her fiancé.

At first glance it seems she's looking to him for some form of confirmation. To the uneducated, it seems as if she's seeking some sign of what to do from her man, but Remo picks up on something else. He knows that look. It can be easily misinterpreted, but Remo sees right through it. Cloris doesn't need a damn thing from Lester in the way of confirmation. No. She's not looking for direction from her man, she's reading him. She's studying Lester. Picking his body language, his eyes, his expression apart to see if this is the same guy she fell in love with or if he's something else. Something she wants or doesn't want. Remo thinks of what Lester said last night.

About killing her.

About her killing all of them.

Did she stay up all night thinking about similar things?

Is she losing trust in Lester, or is Lester the only thing she does trust?

There's a lot going on behind those eyes of hers and Remo would be a fool to think he can decode it all, let alone trust any of it. Cloris isn't someone who's an easy read and Remo, despite all of his faults, is not a fool. Immature, impulsive and a complete asshole, but foolish Remo is not.

Cloris allows a smirk to break as she stands. "Let's do some work, bitches."

She extends a hand to Hollis. They shake with smiles. Somewhat guarded, fake, plastered-on smiles, but smiles nonetheless. She then hugs Lester, squeezing as tight as she can. Remo watches, letting his shoulders ease down, allowing his body to exhale. It might not all be honest, but it's better than a knife fight.

"Great. Great," Remo repeats, trying to convince himself everything is going to be fine.

Peace among the team.

For the moment at least.

CHAPTER ELEVEN

THE TEAM of four stands in the living room, locked and loaded.

Ready to fight a war.

They are riddled with questions and they have little in the way of answers, but being armed seems to soothe some of the doubt. Glocks are tucked in shoulder holsters. Pistol-grip assault shotguns are slung over their backs. Kevlar vests strapped on tight and ARs placed in hand. Bullets, shells and magazines have been evenly distributed and secured.

Remo looks around to his team. He'll think of them as a team for lack of a better name, but he realizes they are far from united. The term *team* works better than thinking of them as Remo's Fun Bunch Death Squad That Can Barely Stand One Another. He did, briefly, think about giving them a proper name for the sake of unity. Maybe the War Eagles or Death from Above or simply Bad Motherfuckers, but nothing was gaining any traction in his mind, and he didn't see the need to put it up for a vote and muddy the already murky-as-fuck waters.

This isn't that type of deal.

There are no cheerleaders here.

No rah-rah shit up in here.

This is a team of rough and tumble folks who don't trust one another and, under any other circumstances, would rather kill each other than work together. Save, of course, for Cloris and Lester, but even those two might kill one another if this situation tilts a certain way. There are a lot of *ifs* floating around. Lester without question would off Cloris and even stated it as such. Remo isn't so sure about Cloris. She's the wild card. Love 'em, or kill 'em all? She might indeed murder every single one of them and grind their bones to toothpicks.

Who knows?

Not knowing is part of the journey, right?

"Fuck," Remo whispers to himself.

The only positive thing here is the fact everyone wants the same thing. There is a single want and need shared by all.

A common goal.

It's the one true binding agent of any team that's worth a shit.

For this team the common goal is plain, old-fashioned self-preservation. Self-preservation is stronger than oak, tougher than steel, and by God self-preservation is what is going to keep this ultra-psychotic, powder keg of unstable death machines in line. That can and should be enough to unite them.

At least that's what Remo is going with.

"All dressed up and nowhere to go," Remo jokes.

No one is laughing or smiling. Only blank looks and blinks fire off from his fully-armed traveling companions.

"We have somewhere to go," Cloris says with bite.

"Yeah. Really?" Hollis snaps.

"What do you mean, Remo?" asks Lester.

"It was a joke, people. An expression. I fucking know fucking have somewhere to go. What I'm saying is I don't know where we are going dressed like we're going to attack Tony Montana's mountain getaway."

"Well, why didn't you just say that?" Cloris says, again with bite.

"Yeah, what's with the bullshit?" Hollis snaps.

"It's just kind of confusing. Can you say what you mean next time, Remo?" asks Lester.

Remo shakes his head, watching the other three exit the house onto the porch. A new concern spikes up from his anus, rocketing toward his mind. Has the common ground among them changed? Has it? It can't be. Nah, things can't go like that so quickly. Can it? Has the new true binding agent for this team become mocking Remo?

No.

This will not do.

Not by a damn sight.

As much as Remo wants the team to come together, being a dick to Remo, the leader, even if no one other than Remo has decided Remo is the leader, will not do. Being a dick to Remo is no way to start this adventure. It's damned divisive. Not binding at all.

"Fuck," Remo whispers to himself.

He stops cold.

Another thought slaps him. This one is more troubling than the previous thought. Much more disturbing than the notion that his new team—that's right, HIS team—is bonding over being unbridled dicks to him.

No. This new thought is worse.

Much worse.

This new thought needs to be resolved. As in now.

Remo sets down the AR and removes his shotgun, then staggers around the room like a frightened boy searching for his lost woobie. His mind fires off the most horrific of ideas. Panic rolling in like the strongest of tides. Hands shake. Head quakes. He flings couch cushions across the room. Shoves the coffee table aside. This thought that just occurred to Remo, but it's growing like an unstoppable tumor and it's the type of idea that can, and will, bury a man like Remo.

Catastrophic, if it is proven to be reality.

This can't be happening.

Remo fling-tosses the bearskin against the wall.

Good God no.

He races to the kitchen, throwing open cabinets left and right. Swings the refrigerator door open wide, letting it slam against the wall.

Sweat begins to bead along his forehead. His heart rate is redlining. His hands shake more and more as an emotional earthquake shutters and rumbles inside of him. His back hits the kitchen wall. Sliding down to the floor, his eyes glaze over, forming lifeless pinholes looking out into the void. A thousand-yard stare sets in. Face a statue of fear.

Hollis steps in, taking note of Remo's feeble, fragile state. He starts to say something, stops, swallows, winces, then asks, "You okay, man?"

Remo mouths some words but no sound comes out.

"What?" Hollis asks.

More inaudible sounds from Remo.

Hollis leans down, getting closer.

"Where's the Johnnie Blue?" Remo says, grabbing Hollis by the collar. "Where's the Blue and the fucking Adderall?"

HIS SUFFERING IS THE KEY

Part II

CHAPTER TWELVE

HOLLIS HELPS Remo out the door and onto the porch, carrying him like a wounded soldier.

He sets him down in the rocking chair, letting him sink into the old, worn wood. Rocking gently back and forth, Remo's stare out into nothingness looks like that of a mental patient. The mountain air feels nice. There's a part of Remo that acknowledges it, but he's still melting down inside and that cannot be derailed by the niceties provided by Mother Nature.

"He gonna make it?" Cloris asks.

Hollis shrugs, then steps back inside to grab Remo's guns.

Lester takes a knee next to Remo as if he were consoling a dying man bound to a wheelchair. He touches his friend's hand and says, "It's all a bit much, isn't it? I know you're not a church man, but I find strength in the words." He pulls his Bible from his pack then thumbs to a certain spot. "Here. You'll dig this one." He reads, "Even though I walk through the darkest valley, I will fear no evil, for you are with me. Your rod and your staff, they comfort me."

Nothing from Remo.

Cloris can't believe what she's seeing.

She's watching her man, her master of disaster, quoting scripture in a caring, moving way. More to the point, he's quoting the word of the Lord in a caring, moving way toward the attorney who fucked him over and killed her brothers.

"Your rod and your staff, asshole," Hollis says, dropping the AR and shotgun on Remo's lap.

"What happened?" asks Lester.

"CIA doesn't supply booze and pills," Hollis says.

"Ooooo." Cloris sucks in through her teeth. "That fuckin' sucks, bro."

Lester thumbs through the pages, finding another verse. "Watch and pray so that you will not fall into temptation. The spirit is willing, but the flesh is weak."

Remo's eyes slip over to Lester.

"I think it's working," Lester says.

Remo's lips part. He whispers, "Lester?"

"Yes, Remo."

"Kill me."

"No, Remo."

"You told me once you were on a mission of mercy."

"I did and I am."

"Then I'm asking for you to shoot me. Now."

"Not what I meant."

"Then fuck the fuck off."

Cloris leans in and slaps the shit out of Remo.

Spit flies. Remo's lips immediately swell as the side of his face throbs. He can feel the heat of his skin trying to work itself back to normal. Cloris grabs Remo by the face, twisting it left and right, up and down, all while holding eye contact.

"I've got no scripture for you, jerkoff. No words of wisdom, comfort or salvation." Cloris moves in even closer to Remo's face, their noses almost touching. "What I've got, all I've got, is a job to do, and you're a part of that job. A big part. I can't do it without you, Remo. *We* can't do it without you."

Remo glances to Lester and Hollis, looking for their assistance.

There is none.

They stand a healthy distance away, both sharing a look of understood helplessness. As if watching the final minutes of a game where the score is 58 to 10. It's over, but it's not.

Cloris yanks Remo's face back over to hers. "You say these are your friends, then be one for fuck's sake. You say you love your son..."

Something inside Remo comes unhinged.

Like a lightning strike went off inside him.

He slaps her hands back and stands, letting the guns slip to the porch but staying in her face. His eyes locked on hers. Burning. Neither backing down.

"That's got nothing to do with you," Remo says.

"It's got everything to do with—"

"No. You don't talk about my son. Got shit to do with you."

"Good. So you do care about something. One thing, at least. Me? My one thing?" She looks over at Lester. "That's mine." She scrunches her nose at Hollis. "Fuck that guy."

Hollis puts his hands up. *What did I do?*

Cloris turns back to Remo. "You done with the alcoholic self-pity bit?" She raises her eyebrows and nods, trying to draw a confirmation from Remo.

He closes his eyes, then nods.

Cloris smiles. She bends down to the porch, thumps Remo's pecker with a flick of her finger, then picks up his guns and hands them to him. Remo takes the guns, ignores the pecker thump best he can, and tries to forget about his chemical needs.

Cloris steps back, points out in the distance like she's calling her shot. She's pointing toward a road that leads like a winding serpent into the mountains. There's a black Yukon parked at the base of the road. She turns back, checking out the faces of the team, smiles and shows them the keys in her hand.

They all share eyes.

Undefined looks flickering back and forth between them.

The same questions rip through all three of them: *How long did she have keys to that thing? What else is she not telling them? And, of course, what the fuck?*

Cloris steps off the porch, letting her foot crunch into the gravel and dirt. She slinks toward the Yukon like a heavily armed goddess of war. Hollis shrugs. Lester chews the inside of his cheek. Remo feels like he's falling off a cliff. His stomach drops. He feels sick as hell. Fresh out of good options, they each fall in behind her one by one, walking a line toward the Yukon. Not a word spoken. None needed.

They have reached a silent understanding.

We need her.

She's trouble.

We're fucked.

CHAPTER THIRTEEN

"Now that we're all friendly," Remo says, "could you please enlighten me as to what in the good fuck we're marching into?"

They've been huffing it up this road for some time now. To be fair, it turned into a dirt path a long time ago, and the team is starting to show signs of fatigue. They ditched the Yukon after the road narrowed and changed to dirt, rock and brush. Cloris said something about needing to be on foot for this part. Since then she's been leading them upward and onward as if she's heading toward the new gold rush. Pausing only briefly to grab ahold of Lester's hand occasionally. Thankfully, the temperature has been doing them a huge favor by not opening up the whoop-ass, but the sun has been shining down hard like God's spotlight for the hour or so they've been walking.

They've remained in silence for most of the trip. This journey into the heart of darkness. This team. This fellowship of questionable people. None of them felt the need to communicate during the drive up, and no one thought it was a great idea to ask questions when Cloris threw the Yukon in park behind some trees and led them up and into this insanely steep motherfucker of a path.

Remo, having endured the early stages of all sorts of with-drawal, is currently dealing with his own personal hell, and isn't enjoying this experience.

Not one damn bit.

The lack of booze and pills is not helping his mood or his ability to tackle a difficult physical activity with a smile. The shakes stopped about ten minutes ago, but he's sure they will be back with a vengeance. Sweat pours from his pores. It coats his skin and stings his eyes, no matter the cool mountain breeze. He can feel the red veins plumping up along his eyes. There's this unnerving sensation, as if ants are crawling all over the rest of him. Wiggling. Dancing. Having a little ant orgy. It escalates. The nonexistent ant horde sex party takes things up a notch. It's as if the ants got bored with doing each other and called in some fleas and ticks to spice things up a bit.

His left ear has clogged up as if someone jammed a doorstop inside it.

His mouth is dry as a drum.

His feet are swelling up to Hobbit-style proportions.

All of this is to say that Remo is not happy.

He's done. Done with this passive-aggressive silent treatment.

Done with playing nice. Just flat-out over the whole fucking thing.

"Cloris, I was addressing you with that question just a second ago. You. I was asking you. In case you were wondering," Remo says, pressing his agenda again. "Should I repeat it? Ask in a different way? More profanity perhaps? Less? Draw some pictures?"

Cloris tries to ignore him, but Lester can tell she's showing signs of breaking down. Remo has a way of doing that to people. Even people as tough to crack as Cloris.

"Cloris? I'm back here." Remo continues to dig at her.

She breathes deeply, bringing in long pulls of air through her nose. Her eyes burn. She feels her shoulders tense. Her body tightens.

"Cloris, no really, I'd like a word."

Cloris seethes.

"Perhaps I should bark or grunt in an attempt to mimic the native tongue of your fucked-up people."

Cloris spins around like an anger-fueled top. She jams her 9 mm between Remo's teeth. Her eyes pop wide. Crazy-person bulging. She breathes deeply in and out through her nose as she presses the gun deeper down Remo's throat. He starts to gag. Lester tries to pull her back. She slaps him back with a free hand.

Hollis pulls his gun, leveling it on her face.

Cloris shoots Hollis the finger then pushes her gun down harder. Deeper down Remo's throat.

He gags. His eyes water.

Cloris giggles.

Her face drops as she feels cold steel pressed against her temple.

Turning slightly, she finds Lester is holding his gun against her head. She can't believe it. Her expression flashes to that of a lost woman. Betrayal washes over her. Betrayed by the man she loves.

"I'm sorry, Buttercup," Lester says. "Need you to remove that gun from his mouth."

"Why?" she asks softly.

"I'm here to save him."

Cloris's eyes drift. It's hitting her now. She finally sees what she thought wasn't so. She wasn't sure before, maybe didn't want to truly consider it as a possibility. But now, with a gun to her head, she has no choice but to deal with the idea as a full-fledged reality.

Has she really lost him?

Is that possible?

This is not the man she knew. Clearly. Something has shifted him into this thing she can't understand. This... whatever he is now. This imposter posing like her Lester. She looks to Remo.

Remo winks at her.

He did this, she thinks. Not sure how, but she knows this lawyer, this fucker is responsible. The thought of pulling the trigger and blowing Remo's face away just on principle flashes across her mind, but she thinks better of it. Cloris removes her gun from his mouth, wipes the spit across Remo's chest, then returns it to its holster.

Lester lowers his weapon.

Hollis follows suit.

Everyone breathes normally again.

Remo can't help but smile. Feel a little giddy. His small victory.

The team is his again.

"We've got a little ways to go, but we're not that far," Cloris says with her head down. "There's a place up the road we can regroup, talk and form a plan or whatever." She looks up to Remo. "You asked what we are marching into?"

Remo nods, still grinning.

"Not sure. Never been inside. Daddy has been putting that place together for some time. A compound of sorts. A command center." Cloris locks into Remo's eyes. "You, Remo, you're our way in. They want you to die and die horribly for what you've done. What you did to my brothers and, more importantly, with the money. Cormac knew this, and that's why he came at you. You see, your suffering is the key to unlock the front door."

Remo swallows hard.

Cloris turns around, heading back up the path. "Come on now."

Hollis shrugs.

Lester puts a hand on Remo's shoulder. "It'll be fine."

Remo wishes the team would go back to not talking.

CHAPTER FOURTEEN

THE TEAM SITS on some large rocks overlooking a mountain view. The vastness.

The scope.

The overwhelming sight of blue skies, rolling clouds, forests of trees spanning up and around the towering monuments of former volcanic activity. Millions of years of nature's effort, front and center. It's a gorgeous sight to soak in, even for this crew.

Cloris sits perched on a massive stone with her eyes closed, letting the sun work its touch over her face. The winds gently run their fingers through her hair. A woman at complete peace. Lost in the moment. Letting her thoughts and concerns float and drift away. Lester watches her. Hard to get his read on the situation. He admires the Lord's wonderful canvas too, but Lester is still troubled by one of the Lord's children. One of the Lord's bat-shit crazy children. The one he's convinced will try to kill them all.

Hollis gets up, unzips and begins pissing on a tree.

The peacefulness of the surroundings do not match what's churning around inside Remo. In addition to really, really wanting a drink, he has Cloris's last statement rattling around in his skull.

"His suffering is the key."

That's what that woman actually said.
Remo watches her. Like Lester, but in a different way. He's trying to decode. Seems like he's spending a lot of time recently trying to crack this Cloris. She talked about Cormac using Remo for this. Using him to pull this team together, even if Remo didn't know he was doing it.
What the hell is the deal with Cormac?
Why is the CIA all over us?
Remo can think of several things, but nothing concrete. Earlier he thought it was only Crow back in NYC. He'd heard Crow had some dealings with gunrunners. Some international money laundering stuff. Nothing too insane, but maybe enough to get the CIA involved.
Maybe.
But not at this level. Not to this extent.
No way.
Cormac brought in a group of civilians to kill people. That's more than a garden-variety crime boy dipping his wick in international waters. Crow, at the max, was a mid-level crime lord with a fraction of his business overseas.
The Mashburns?
Are the Mashburns what Cormac has such a hard-on for?
Remo thinks hard. Punching and pulling away at the cobwebs of his mind. Moving old furniture and boxes out of the way in the dusty attic of his memory. He tries to remember if there was anything in the Mashburns' files that would bring in the CIA. Anything in their history that would bring in this brand of high heat.
Nope.
Nothing.
The Mashburns were all about smash-and-grab jobs. Banks. Armored car takedowns. They'd work over some drug dealers here and there. Move some powder. Roll a stash house. He heard about Chicken Wing going apeshit at a strip joint once. Dutch

put a bouncer at a biker bar in a coma, while Ferris lit a bartender on fire. All crimes, sure, but nothing on a global scale. No immediate, external threat or clear and present danger to the security of these United States.

Maybe that's what's going on at this compound.

Maybe there's some big-time, big-money, international crime shit going on in there, and the Mashburn brothers and Cloris were on the outside of it all. Daddy Mashburn knew not to involve those wild cards in his bigger plans. They would only fuck things up, and Daddy Mashburn didn't want any of that.

Maybe this Daddy Mashburn is a global crime lord who slipped under the radar. The white whale of the law enforcement community. People like Cormac have been on him for years, but could never get their hands on him. Chasing. Fighting. Scouring the earth to find a way to bring this mastermind to justice, and now Remo is the key to making America safe again. That's right, Remo-Captain-Mother-Fucking-America-Cobb is here to make things right. Sleep safe kids. Remo's got this.

Remo stands up on top of his rock, letting the wind's fingers work through his hair.

His chest out.

He wishes he had a cape.

"You're so fucked," Hollis says, shaking his dick then zipping his fly. "These whacky psycho bastards are going to eat your liver, shit it out and feed it back to you."

Remo sits back down.

Thinks. Rubs his face.

Fuck.

Resets and reassesses the situation.

Remo scrambles up from his rock and hauls ass into the woods.

CHAPTER FIFTEEN

"Do we have a plan?" Remo asks as he picks a twig out from of his ear.

Cloris and the rest of the team side-eye a pissed off glance his way as they gather their weapons. None of them are happy with Remo at the moment. None of them wanted to drop everything and chase him out into the wild. He didn't make if very far, but still, it was an energy burn, and once they got to him he had a pretty embarrassing meltdown. There weren't any tears, but there was screaming, random profanity and panic.

Lots of panic.

Okay, fine, there were tears.

A lot of them.

Snot, too.

Cloris dove-tackled him to the ground after Remo made it about twenty yards or so into the thick trees. They rolled, tumbled and fought. Well, Remo tried to fight. He swung hard. Made it look good for a second or two. Then Cloris punched him in the nose. Only once. The fight ended shortly after it started. Lester then picked him up and carried him back down to where they were sitting. Hollis called Remo a dumbass and mumbled something about fucking hating him.

Remo recognized that he panicked. He even apologized, which is something he doesn't do on a regular basis, and said he was fine now. Just a momentary lapse of reason. *It will never happen again*, he said. He explained that it's been a rough few days, plus him giving up the booze and the pills has caused him to not be himself. He said he won't do it again, won't even think about doing it again, and that they could count on it. Trust him. Take it to the bank. Remo is solid.

Then he ran like a child toward the woods, his arms flailing.

That time Hollis put out his forearm and clotheslined Remo in the throat, putting him on his back before he could make it very far.

Cloris appreciated that.

They are now all seated back on their respective rocks. Back to letting the wind's fingers work their hair. This time Hollis and Remo share a rock. Just in case.

"Because if we've got one, I'd love to hear it. Your plan," Remo says, picking a bug out of his shirt. "I mean some plan other than my suffering being the main focus of it."

"It's only fair," Lester says to Cloris. "Not only to Remo, but to all of us to know what you're thinking, here."

"Yeah," Hollis says. "We need to know what you know."

Cloris lets her eyes glide over all of them. Taking in each of their faces. She sighs, letting her shoulders drop. "I don't know much," she says. "I know Daddy's been working on this for a while. I know there are probably a lot of tough boys up in there, and I know they'll want Remo. Like in a bad kind of way."

"You're his daughter," Remo says. "Why can't you just walk in there and talk to these animals?"

"Because I left when Daddy probably needed me the most. The cops were all over us. His boys slipped up. Couple dead and one headed to prison, or so we thought," Cloris explains. "Also, I told him to fuck off the last time we spoke."

"Oh, good," Remo says.

"Smart," Hollis says.

Lester thinks it's better to stay out of this.

"Never heard anything about Daddy Mashburn while I was on the brothers' case," Remo says. "Never saw a file or any kind of record or any mention of him."

"He's never been caught," Cloris says.

"Never? How's that possible?" Remo asks.

"He's pretty good at shit," she says.

"Also means he doesn't leave loose ends," Hollis says, thinking out loud. "Witnesses get gone quick. He keeps his people close and kills the ones he thinks might turn and, oh yeah, he hides in the mountains like a frightened little bitch."

"Daddy doesn't hide," Cloris fires back.

Hollis nods, letting it go. He's learning how to talk to her. Picking up on where to go and where not to. He looks to Remo. Remo picks up on it too.

"So, Cloris, what *is* your plan?" Remo asks again. "Please share. I'm guessing you need me as a peace offering of sorts. That the thing?"

Cloris nods.

"That's how I'm the key to the front door?"

She nods again.

"Then what?" Remo asks.

She shrugs.

Remo shrugs back, mocking her.

She shrugs again with a *fuck you* smile this time.

"Really," Remo says, "that's what you've got? Well fuck me all over the place. That is some amazing shit you've got there."

Lester puts a calming hand on Remo. Cloris giggles.

"Well," Hollis chimes in, "how far out can they see us? I mean do they know we're here?"

She shrugs.

"Can you join the fucking conversation?" Remo asks.

"I don't know," Cloris says. "Daddy's not a huge technology guy, but he's got people who are. I picked this spot to hang because I thought it was far enough out. Based on what I know about the old place, this was a good distance away. By at least a couple hundred yards or so."

Lester looks around. "Good tree coverage too. Not sure he's got the tech to see us here."

"Okay," Hollis starts up again. "Let's assume they don't have eyes on us. Our best bet is to have you take Remo in. A peace offering from his daughter. You've been away and you were an ungrateful child, but you're back with a prize. A gift for Daddy. You're offering up that slimy, piece of shit dickhole who killed your brothers."

"Easy now," Remo says.

Cloris is all ears, liking what she's hearing.

Lester leans in, digging what Hollis is laying down.

"Once you're in," Hollis says, "Lester and I will give it ten minutes and come in with guns blazing."

Silent beat. The breeze blows.

Cloris scrunches her nose. "That it?"

"Yeah, that's it," Hollis says with a look of pride.

"Kinda lean, don't ya think?" she says.

"Not much of plan," Lester says.

"I've heard this plan," Remo says. "It's the same bullshit plan you had with Crow in New York, and you didn't fucking show. I almost got killed. Shit, man. I almost killed myself for fuck's sake."

"It was a good plan then, and it's a good plan now. Daddy Mashburn's people are going to search you, just like at Crow's, so you can't contact us and tell us where to go or what the situation is. Not to mention," Hollis says, tilting his head toward Cloris, "she's the one who fucked the Crow thing all up."

Lester nods.

"Me?" Cloris chirps.

"Yes, you. You beat the piss out of me and your boy with a two by four and left us facedown in an alley right before we were headed in to save this fucking prick."

Remo holds his hands out. *What the fuck, man?*

"How in the hell was I supposed to know that shit?" she says.

"Well, she's here now at least, and she can't fuck this one up," Lester says, pauses, then, "yet."

Cloris fires him a look. Lester shuts down, realizing his stupidity. He goes with the proven method of slumping over with eyes looking toward the ground.

"Seven," Remo says. "Seven minutes."

"Why seven?" Cloris asks.

"Better than ten," Remo says.

"Why not six or eight?" she asks.

"Don't be stupid," Remo says.

Lester puts a hand out, holding back Cloris.

"Fine. Fuck it," Hollis says. "Seven minutes and we'll come in."

Hollis looks around the circle. Slowly the nods roll in, one by one. They are all in, more or less. The team of four sits in silence. Each of them staring out over the mountain view. Just as gorgeous as it was before they started this conversation, before Remo tried to haul ass away, but it doesn't have the same feeling as it did a few minutes ago. A bird soars. The breeze blows. The sun shines down on them.

"You better fucking show this time," Remo mutters.

"Don't doubt my shit, fuckhead," Hollis says.

More silence.

Cloris holds Lester's hand. He lets her. He tries to not like it. Cloris shares a flash of eyes with him. Sparks a dangerous thought. A feeling. A feeling that there's still a place for her in there somewhere. Something inside Lester still wants her. Wants this. Remo sees all this. Lester senses Remo's questioning look and drops her hand.

Cloris rolls her eyes. *Why is this so damn difficult?*

"What about the kill squad?" Lester asks. "What about Cormac's people?"

Cloris is pissed about the hand dropping but lets it go, for the moment.

"I can't signal them in until I know where Daddy Mashburn is," Remo says. "They gave me this thing." He pulls a tiny device from his chest pocket. "I'm going to hide it under my ball sack."

Cloris winces in disgust, like she swallowed a bug.

"Oh, excuse me, *delicate flower*," Remo snips. "Why don't you try fucking the faith out of Lester again."

Cloris pops up. Lester holds her back, again. He knows if she wanted to she could easily bust through is arm block. She sits back down, but still pissed.

"When I find him," Remo continues, now speaking directly at Cloris, "I remove the device from under my sweaty beanbag and crack it open. That will send a signal out and then they come riding in like cowboys from hell."

"Okay. So what if you see him in the first minute?" Hollis asks.

"What?" Remo fires back.

"Well, if the kill squad comes riding in, " Hollis says, "should we still wait ten—"

"Seven," Remo says.

"Sorry, seven. Should we still wait seven minutes?"

Remo leans back on that one. The rest of the team share looks. None of them know. Not for sure.

"How about this." Remo stands. "Seven minutes unless you hear some serious shit going down."

"Do I get a definition of *serious shit?*" Hollis asks.

"Yeah, that one's a little vague," Cloris says.

"Yeah," Lester adds.

"Gunshots," Remo says. "If you hear gunshots you should engage."

"As in multiple?" Hollis ask.

"No, one, motherfucker," Remo barks. "You hear one gunshot you need to storm in directly."

Hollis thinks, then looks over, raising his eyebrows to Lester as if silently asking, *You cool with this?* Lester puts his hands up, nodding as if to say, *Sure, fuck it.*

They both look to Remo and give him the nod.

Remo gives a half-smirk to Cloris. It's still his team, dammit.

Cloris throws him a stare that would kill a thousand people in their tracks. Hollis and Lester start packing up their weapons, not paying attention to the little moment Remo and Cloris are having between them.

Remo sits, frozen off Cloris's crazed expression.

Cloris swipes her finger across her throat and blows him a kiss.

Remo swallows and remembers a fact he'd forgotten. Something he should never forget. He's a complete asshole and he cannot, will not, allow a Mashburn to out asshole him.

He stands, unzips, drops his pants, raises his ball sack ever so slightly then sticks the CIA device safely underneath his boys. All this with a goofy-as-hell smile plastered on his face, never allowing his eye contact with Cloris to break.

Her expression fades. Chin drops. Her eyes burn.

"Remo, dude." Hollis sighs. "Enough with the balls."

CHAPTER SIXTEEN

CLORIS AND REMO push their way up a steep incline.

The area is thick with trees and brush. The rocky ground makes for tricky travel, seconds away from turning an ankle or landing face-first in the dirt.

Feels like it's hard to find enough air to suck in.

Their lungs burn. Hurts to breathe.

The dirt path that once resembled a road disappeared about an hour ago. It's been straight slogging up through the wild ever since. Cloris removed Remo's guns and handed them off to Lester and Hollis to hang on to. An armed Remo doesn't fit the narrative. Besides, she likes him feeling defenseless as hell. Makes her happy.

Their thighs burn. Calves balled up hard like concrete. Remo's limbs feel the spike of pain much more than hers. She's got younger muscles and joints and probably, even though he'd never admit it, she is simply a better athlete. One thing they share is the shortness of breath. The higher altitude, along with the physical demands of huffing it up the mountain, is wearing them both down fast. Their labored breath plumes out in front of their mouths. Each one is harder and harder to draw in and out. The temperature seems to have dropped dramatically since they started this climb.

The good news?

Remo has long forgotten about his alcohol and pill withdrawal issues. That time has passed. It's hard now for him to separate the physical pain caused by this little adventure and the longing for booze and big pharma. Everything hurts. Life is simply one big ball of hurt. His limbs, his lungs, his brain and pounding heart are all demanding his attention and sympathy, regardless of the cause.

"How much more of this shit?" Remo asks.

"Not much," Cloris says. "I think."

"There has to be another way up here. A road or something. This is insane."

"Nope. No other way."

"This sucks."

"Think it sucks now, wait 'til we get there."

That shut Remo up. He had almost forgotten for a minute where they were headed. Truth is, this isn't much fun for her either, but she'll never let Remo know how much she's hurting too. Fuck that. She'd rather die before admitting weakness to this man. This *lawyer*.

She places a hand on a tree, feeling for something in the bark. Looking up and around, there's something she recognizes. The place, the compound, it's close. So close. She stares up along a row of trees, then looks behind her, and then up ahead again. Yeah, she knows it's not far now. Cloris stops Remo and pulls out a set of zip tie handcuffs. Remo's eyes pop wide.

"Fuck. That," he says.

"Got to, bro."

"No, *bro*, ya really don't."

"Think. Am I really supposed to make them believe I've tracked you down and dragged you in from New York without any kind of restraint? You think that tells a convincing story? Oh yeah..."

She punches Remo in the nose, then the eye, and then the nose again. Remo stumbles back holding his swelling face. Blood slipping through his fingers.

"What the fuck, lady!" Remo yelps.

"Gotta look good. Look like you put up a fight."

"Couldn't try convincing them with your words? Fuck!" he says, struggling to hold back his beaten-down man-tears.

She rolls her eyes. *This fucking guy's killing me.*

She wishes Lester were here with her now. He'd talk some sense into this asshole. This asshole *lawyer.* Lester and Hollis are staying back a bit, letting Cloris and Remo make their way, and then advancing forward bit by bit so they don't trigger any attention. According to the finer points of the plan, Lester and Hollis have stopped a ways back. Out of sight. Keeping a safe distance from where Cloris thinks the compound is located.

"Trust, Remo. Trust me," Cloris says, holding out the zip ties. "This is all about trust. You trusting me, and them trusting that I'm doing what I tell them I'm doing."

Remo listens, but doesn't offer up his hands for the ties either.

"If they don't believe our story, then this thing is over before it starts. They will kill us both," she says.

"You think they'd kill you too?"

"It's a strong possibility. They'll kick the shit out of me and throw me in a hole at the minimum."

She takes his hands in hers and speaks softly. "This is it. Up there not much farther is a house, perhaps a fortress, full of people who want to pull you to pieces. If you bolt, the CIA will pull you to pieces. The only thing stopping both of those things from happening is me and the two guys back there."

Remo knows damn well she's right. He hates it, but knows everything she's saying is true. Trusting is not something that comes easily to a man like Remo. In his defense, he hasn't had much reason to trust anyone, given the company he's kept.

Certainly no reason to trust this woman, but he knows he really has no choice.

He gives a defeated nod, offering up his wrists to her.

Cloris mouths a silent *thank you* then slips the zip ties over his wrists, securing them tightly. "Used to use these all the time on Lester, " she says, then spanks Remo's ass hard as she can. "Before he found Jesus and shit."

Remo swallows hard, pushing some blood down his throat.

He remembers Lester's concerns about Cloris killing all of them. There's this look in her eyes. It comes and goes. Hard to tell what triggers it exactly. There have been times when the trigger was obvious. When she wanted to kill Hollis at dinner that look in her eyes made perfect sense, but it's here now too. Like it's this wandering wave of whacko that comes and goes with the wind. Sometimes it makes some sense, but most of the time it's just plain fucking whacko for the sake of being whacko. Remo wonders if there's a way to harness that power. To bottle up her whacko and release it when necessary, like popping a bottle of bubbly on special occasions. He wonders if Lester knows that's not possible. Maybe he's tried. Remo wonders if this is why Lester thinks she will kill them all. Then realizes how pointless it is to wonder while being zip-tied by a crazy person.

"Shit," Remo mutters to himself.

Cloris grabs him by the cuffs and leads Remo upward and onward. This is the hardest part of their trip. Remo is completely relying on Cloris to help him balance and move. He can barely use his upper body and certainly can't use his hands because of the zip ties. Didn't think it was possible, but it seems as if the terrain has actually gotten steeper and more challenging. Harder and harder to churn their thighs upward and onward. They huff and puff for maybe twenty more minutes and then Remo stops.

His feet stick in the ground like a statue.

He sees it.

Up just above a ridge of rocks and behind some trees is a

fence. A big one. A seven-foot high fence made of steel with razor wire protecting its top. Cloris stops as well, but her awe has more of a sense of appreciation to it than Remo's *what the fuck* expression. This is the first time she's seen it too. The first time she's seen it as a fully realized thing. Her daddy had talked and talked about it. It was a dream of his to construct a command center in the mountains. Cloris thought her daddy had watched too many Bond movies and wanted an evil lair. Maybe she was right, but it is a sight to see in the flesh. She can't help but be taken aback by the reality of her daddy's vision sitting in front of her.

To the uninformed, it looks like a really nice mountain getaway for the rich and famous. Maybe a lodge of sorts. Wood and stone accent the walls and the roof appears to be made of metal. Of course the razor wire on top of the fence takes some of the hominess off of the place, but it does have an "upscale cabin out in the woods" vibe to it. The fence seems to be a box, with the edges cutting back toward the east and west. What Cloris and Remo are standing in front of seems to be the main entrance of the place, measuring about half a football field wide.

From the angle they are standing at they can see the upper portion of the place. The second floor. Might even be the third. They can't see it all because of the fence, but the place does seem huge. As if a mansion had been dropped by helicopter on the side of the mountain.

Remo sees a beefy bastard with a sniper rifle on the deck.

Jumping back, Remo tries to hide behind a tree.

Cloris sees the beefy sniper too. She smiles and turns to Remo. "Oh, that's Ronnie. He's cool. Worked for Daddy for years. Just stick with me and he shouldn't put a bullet in your skull."

There's a flurry of crunches on the ground. Whiffs of tree limbs.

They both freeze, stopping dead in their tracks.

Feels like the sounds are rushing toward them from all directions. Something or someone is moving their way fast.

No time to run or hide. The sounds are closing in. Rolling on top of them.

Before Remo can process exactly what's happening, a blur of humanity blankets them, surrounding them in a circle. Guns, too many to count, leveled at their heads. A shotgun barrel rests on Remo's nose.

The silence booms.

Time crawls.

Seconds seem like hours.

A bird chirps.

A massive man with head void of hair moves in, parting the gun-toting crowd that has wrapped around Remo and Cloris.

Cloris giggles. "Hi, Daddy."

BEFORE THE MONSTER RIPS YOU APART

Part III

CHAPTER SEVENTEEN

HOLLIS AND LESTER have taken positions among the trees.

Lester is hidden behind a wide spruce.

Hollis has climbed up the same tree, perching himself on a large limb with an ideal sightline. Reminds him of the old days. He's taken the lives of several people while perched like a bird on a limb. Using the scope on his AR as a telescope of sorts, he scans the area straight ahead of him. He's been watching Cloris and Remo best he can through the foliage and wilderness. Seconds ago he witnessed them get bum-rushed by a pack of heavily armed bad guys. There was one, bigger than the rest, who was clearly in charge. Hollis is guessing that is none other than Daddy Mashburn.

Hollis thinks of taking a shot and ending this thing.

Drop Daddy Mashburn right here. Right now.

Places his finger on the trigger, truly considering removing the proverbial head of the snake.

He stops.

He's never fired this particular gun before. Even though he's very familiar with ARs, you never know a weapon until you dance with it a bit. He also knows the odds of pulling off a perfect headshot a hundred-plus yards away through heavy foliage, mountain air and a touch of wind with an unfamiliar assault rifle is a dicey proposition at best.

So he removes his finger from the trigger.

Takes a deep breath, then waves down to Lester, giving him a thumbs-up.

Lester nods and immediately starts his watch's timer to count-down from seven minutes to zero. He returns the thumbs-up to Hollis.

Hollis goes back to watching Cloris and Remo. They are now being lead through the steel gates of the compound. It only opens up a crack for them, just enough for everybody to slip inside the walls. It wasn't much information, but certainly enough for Hollis to understand this wasn't going to be easy. A seven-foot steel fence with razor wire and a steel gate that more than likely has some armed dickheads behind it is a challenge. Also, that pack of bad guys knew Cloris and Remo were there, so they have some kind of sensors or surveillance around the place.

Not the toughest test Hollis has faced, but it's a challenge nonetheless. He immediately starts making some calculations in his battle-brain about the equipment he and Lester have. They have guns, of course, and some explosives. He tries to determine if the charges they have are enough to blow the gate. Of course this doesn't solve the problem of what's behind the gate.

Are there two dozen dickheads in there, or two hundred?

Will the gates fall and Lester and Hollis be met by a wave of bullets?

Will Hollis ever see his wife and kids again?

Hollis shakes his head hard, trying to clear that shit out.

No time to think of them.

Not now.

Cormac slipped him a note when Remo wasn't looking. Hollis hasn't told any of the team about it. Remo would go apeshit. He thinks he's the leader. Don't make Hollis laugh. Hollis has strug-gled with keeping the Cormac note from them since the second it was handed to him. He doesn't like secrets among his team. For many reasons, Hollis is still a man of his word, and believes in being straight with people, especially those he's going to war with. To be clear, for better or worse Lester, Cloris and Remo qualify. They are a team. *Dammit.*

Also, Hollis doesn't know if he can trust Cormac in any way, shape or form. Hollis wanted to talk to Remo privately, because Remo seems to be the one who's had the most face time with Cormac. Hollis respects Remo's ability to read people, even though he's been off recently, and Hollis knows Remo to be sharp when playing the people game. There just hasn't been much time for a one-on-one, private conversation.

The note from Cormac simply said: *Kill Daddy Mashburn = Hollis gets his family back.*

Hollis deeply wants this to be true. It's hard for your logical brain to overpower your emotions. He'd kill Daddy Mashburn and a thousand others like him if he could go back. Turn back the clock. Go back to the life he had only a few days ago. A life with his wife and kids. A normal, good life. A life like before Remo came to his door. A life void of Remo? A man can dream.

Fucking Remo.

Hollis continues scanning the area, then stops cold.

Through his scope he sees something.

He has another man in his sights.

Another man with a scope. A beefy bastard. A sniper pointing a McMillan TAC-50 directly at him. Hollis knows this gun too.

Very familiar with it.

"That's disappointing," Hollis whispers.

CHAPTER EIGHTEEN

REMO AND CLORIS are escorted into the compound by Daddy Mashburn and his armed friends.

The gate rolls to a close behind them with a clank of steel that leaves a bone-chilling sound rattling around in Remo's ears. His heart pounds, but he keeps his eyes glued on Cloris. He wants to take in her every move. Wants to know exactly how she acts around these people. Around her father. Her facial expressions. The tone in her voice. These are the things that will help Remo form a moderately informed decision about her.

Is she nervous?

Relaxed, like there's nothing wrong?

More to the point, is she full of shit and playing all of them— Remo, Hollis, Cormac, even Lester? Is her relationship with Daddy Mashburn really strained, or was that all prefabricated bullshit? Perhaps Cormac and Cloris are playing Daddy and the whole fucking lot of them. The possible combinations of mind-fucks Cloris is capable of right now is reaching lotto levels.

Cloris blows Remo a kiss.

Remo's butt puckers.

"You did it, honey," Daddy Mashburn says, giving his special girl a big, special hug. A tear rolls down his smiling face. "You really did it. You found this piece of shit legal eagle cocksucker." Daddy Mashburn jams his sausage finger into Remo's chest. "You have no idea how long I'm going to take killing you."

Remo's stomach drops.

Daddy Mashburn hugs Cloris again. Squeezes her even harder this time.

Remo reaches for his balls. Under his balls, to be exact.

A gunshot cracks from above.

CHAPTER NINETEEN

THE TREE EXPLODES above Hollis's head.

He jumped a fraction of a second before the .50 caliber round turned the upper section of the tree into toothpicks. Tumbling, twisting, crashing, Hollis absorbs every thwap and whip of the limbs on the way down. He hits the open air, freefalling down, down and down.

Hollis thinks of his family again.

What he wouldn't give to get back to them.

Fucking Remo.

As he float-tumbles toward the ground, he shakes Remo from his head and decides now is the perfect time to think of his family. He'd like to have some pleasant thoughts before his body makes impact with the hard earth below him.

He had a fall like this in Hong Kong a few years ago. No trees, but he hit the street hard from roughly the same height. He managed to peel himself off the concrete and kill four people with a fork, but he spent the better part of six months laid up in a hospital afterward. He was younger then. Healed faster then. A man north of forty doesn't snap back that way anymore.

This is going suck so bad, he thinks.

He's fairly sure Cloris fucked them all over.

He whispers an apology to his wife and kids.

Lester catches Hollis, or at least tries to. More like he slows him down slightly by breaking his high-speed tumble to the ground. Hollis slams into Lester like a piano dropped from a building. Lester's knees buckle under the crushing force and weight of Hollis, sending them both down hard to the dirt like a couple two-hundred-pound sacks of sod. It's not pretty. A salad of legs, elbows and arms without grace or a hint of fun, but Hollis is alive and relatively okay. It was painful to be sure, and he'll feel it more tomorrow or later today, but the results of the fall would have been far worse had Lester not been there for him.

As Hollis lies there on top of Lester with his eyes looking skyward, his mind slams into place. He realizes quickly the reality of Lester being there for him. Something very clear hits Hollis like a baseball bat to the face.

Lester risked himself to help Hollis.

This is not something to take lightly.

Hollis and Lester were moments away from killing one another just a few days ago. There was no trust. No bond. No way the two of them even liked one another. Couldn't even hold a simple conversation. But still, Lester risked his well-being to save him.

Hollis knows this is on him.

Knows damn well he should have checked for snipers.

It's the first thing he should have done. He underestimated the enemy and that's a sin that cannot be forgiven where Hollis is from. He's better than that. He let the shitstorm he's currently in with Remo and company cloud his training and experience. He let all the things that have happen with Crow and Cormac, the Mashburns and Cloris, and, yes, fucking Remo, stop him from being what he is—a weapon. A trained man of murder. A certified badass.

Right now, he's a stack of meat and bone laid out on top of a criminal man of the Lord. He allowed all the crazy get the best of him. He allowed a crazy woman to get the upper hand. Both at the house last night and just now. He let the sadness over his family dull his edge. He let the outside world creep into his battle-brain and that shit has to stop. Right fucking now.

Lester grunts something.

"Thank you," Hollis says, almost too quiet to hear.

Lester grunts something that could be *you're welcome*.

"I gotta say two things before I get off of you," Hollis says. "First, I was wrong. You're good people."

Another grunt.

"Second, I think your girl is going to fuck us over."

Silence.

Another gunshot crack sounds from above taking more of the tree apart. Bark and chunks of wood rain down all over them. Hollis rolls, pulling Lester along with him. A massive hunk of tree stabs into the ground where they were lying a half-second ago. Sticks in the ground looking a lot like a wooden tombstone.

Hollis and Lester are now face-to-face. Eyes locked. Goofy grins spread across their faces. It's as if they just communicated telepathically. Something just occurred to them at the exact same time.

"That was two shots," Lester says.

Hollis nods. "Yes, yes it was."

"We were supposed to go in after one."

"We're late."

Lester's eyes flare. "Let's go kill some bad guys."

CHAPTER TWENTY

A SECOND SHOT RIPS, echoing from above.

Remo continues to finger-dig under his balls looking for the device Cormac gave him. It's difficult, given that his hands are cuffed with zip ties, but the CIA death squad is very much needed right now, and their presence would be deeply appreciated.

"You said you would grab the asshole attorney and you did it," Daddy Mashburn says, beaming with pride. "Now, I assume Ronnie is hammering away at some people who tailed you."

His expression slams to ice cold. Takes Cloris off guard.

"People you let track you," he says. "Let track you to here."

His face goes hard. Angry. Blood boiling under the skin.

"Here. You know what this place means to me. How hard I've worked."

Cloris recoils a bit, a child being scolded by her father. Her chin quivers as she says, "I didn't see anybody—"

Daddy Mashburn slaps her to the ground.

Remo takes note while fidgeting with his nuts. Perhaps she didn't fuck them all over. It's possible she's playing a different game.

What the hell is she doing?
Is she playing us or is she playing Daddy?
The CIA?
Or all of us?

Cloris's face bounces off the dirt. Had to hurt like hell, but she manages a smile along with a wink that only Remo can see. *That wasn't a mistake. She knowingly did something, but again, what the hell is she doing?* Remo thinks. He's highly confused by what's going on with Cloris right now, but not half as confused as he is with the fact he can't find that goddamn thing under his hairy beanbag.

"Find who her dumb ass led to us and put 'em in the ground," Daddy Mashburn barks to his boys, then looks down to his daughter. "Thanks for the lawyer, but you're truly a fucking disappointment."

Daddy Mashburn and the others scatter with weapons ready. Two know to stay behind and keep watch on Cloris and Remo. They take positions standing over Cloris with eyes on Remo. They don't know what to make of Remo. They simply watch as he has his cuffed hands jammed down his pants.

"Jesus, man," one of Mashburn's boys says. "Show some class."

Cloris springs up with a tactical SOG knife gripped in her fist. She whips around like a spinning ball of whirling violence that just got her string pulled. Slits both of their throats wide open in one single rip of the blade. Their bodies flop to the ground, necks spitting crimson, dropped and bleeding out in a blink of an eye.

Remo freezes at the sight of it. Stuck on pause.

"Well, get the damn thing already," she says, nodding to his balls.

Remo snaps back to reality. He's getting better with the all the blood, guts and blinding violence being played out in front of him, but it still takes him a second to get unstuck from the sight of it. He goes back to searching his undercarriage. Same results. It's very frustrating. He's doing the best he can, dammit. The zip ties are cutting into him, not to mention his focus has been slowed by all the pumping, spilling blood in front of him. He feels his sweaty boys slip and slide between his struggling digits. Gliding over the tips of his fingers.

"I... I..." he stammers. "My balls. My fingers. I fucking..."

Cloris rolls her eyes.

Pussy.

Wasting no time, she drops to her knees, unzips his pants, and shoves his balls hard upward like she was stowing a carry-on in an overhead bin. It takes a second, but she zeroes in and yanks the device from Remo's trembling crotch. The adhesive gives a rip taking a bit of skin and hair with it. Upon under-nut-release, Remo buckles over. Spins twice then topples over like a bowling pin, landing with his face a few inches from the gushing, recently cut throats.

Cloris closes her eyes. Thinks of Lester.

Whispers a quick prayer. Been a long time, but she thinks she did it right.

She snaps the CIA device in half. With her eyes still closed, as clearly and calmly as can be, she says, "Burn it down," into a tiny round black thing inside the snapped device.

"Come on in, boys," Cloris says as her eyes pop wide open. "Come kill Daddy so I don't have to."

Through the pain Remo recognizes the crazed look in her eyes.

"Fuck me," he whispers.

CHAPTER TWENTY-ONE

LESTER AND HOLLIS move quickly up the mountain.

They try to exercise as much caution as they can manage without reducing the speed of their charge. Lester follows Hollis's lead. He's learning from Hollis. He studies his moves. Hollis makes subtle tilts, takes smooth angles and does not waste movements. These are moves a highly trained killer makes.

Lester is not too proud to learn from others. He would usually charge face-first into this type of situation with guns blazing like he was shoved right into *The Wild Bunch*. Hollis has done that before, but only as a last resort.

Hollis is moving forward, claiming territory inch by inch with his AR scanning the area. He takes a position behind the largest tree he can find.

He nods for Lester.

Lester mimics the move, but passes Hollis, taking a tree about ten yards farther up ahead. They are trying to scan and clear chunks of the landscape while pushing their way toward the compound. As if the two of them were carving up the mountain into manageable bite-size pieces. They can somewhat safely assume the danger is in front of them, so their zone of bad shit is minimized somewhat.

Hollis spins out from the tree as Lester stops. Something catches his eye up ahead. A movement. A sound. Hollis takes his position behind a tree directly next to Lester. Hollis points up ahead. Lester nods then raises his AR along with Hollis. In almost perfect harmony they look through their scopes, pointing in the same direction—the front of the compound.

There's a sound of rolling wheels along metal. They see the gate opening.

Four, armed, tatted-up crime boys rush out.

A large, bald man steps out behind them.

Tilting up, they see the beefy bastard sniper above. Hollis lines him up about to take him out, but stops. The sniper is turning away from their direction. He takes aim to the west side of the compound. Something new has his attention.

Tilting down, Hollis sees the CIA kill squad securing explosive charges to the west-side wall, moments away from breaching the compound.

A wave of rapid-fire bullets carves up the bark and ground around Hollis and Lester. They spin hard back behind their respective trees. They share a glance. Amid the punishing fire-power, the two men who were forced into teamwork, wedged into respect, and jammed into a friendship look to one another. This is it. This is their world. It's not a pretty or perfect or a clean place to live. It's more of the dirty, ugly and shitty variety, but it's a world they've learned to excel in.

They nod.

They spin.

They open fire.

CHAPTER TWENTY-TWO

GUNFIRE ERUPTS BEYOND THE WALL.

Cloris and Remo turn to one another. Eyes wide. Mouths open.

It's starting. They both think of Lester and Hollis out there in the woods.

The west wall explodes.

The CIA kill squad storms in, draped all in black. Every muscle attached to every member has an assignment. A task. Not a single move wasted. Not a breath taken in without a plan. One member of the squad ever so slightly turns upward and fires two controlled bursts of three rounds apiece.

The beefy bastard sniper slumps, falls, then lands to the ground in a broken, bloody mess.

The four-member kill squad rushes in with amazing efficiency toward Cloris and Remo. Like a small pack of highly disciplined wolves. Scanning up, down and around the compound while moving in a spread out, yet still tight formation.

Remo lets his shoulders relax. He feels a huge weight being lifted off his chest. This is almost over. There are a lot of loose ends, and he has to trust somebody he can't trust, meaning

Cormac, but this feels like hope to him, or least a mutated version of it. Hope that he can get out from under this thing. He can leave this all far behind if he can only stay alive. There's hope.

Hope he can have a life with Sean in it.

The kill squad circles Cloris and Remo with one of them, the leader, moving close to Remo, conversation close, but still scanning the area with his HK416 held tight.

"Daddy Mashburn?" the kill squad leader asks Remo.

"He went out the gate," Remo says. "But I have a question."

The leader, completely ignoring Remo, gives a hand motion to his squad. They roll like water, moving on toward the gate. Remo grabs the leader's arm. The leader lands a quick, lightning elbow strike to Remo's nose then jams his HK onto Remo's forehead. The nose strike restarts the blood flow from the tag to the nose he took earlier from Cloris.

"Wait. Shit, man," Remo says, spitting blood but still holding on to his arm. "Tell me. What does the CIA want with me?"

The leader shakes his arm loose.

Remo, despite his better judgment, grabs his arm again. This time he dodges the elbow jab. "Ha, motherfucker."

Two other kill squad members slam him to the ground, putting gun barrels on him.

"He does that again? Shoot him," the leader says.

"Tell me, dammit. What the hell does the CIA want with me? Is it global? Guns? Money laundering? What? What the fuck?" Remo pleads, nearing a breakdown. "Just tell me. I want out. I want a normal, real life."

The leader starts to move away.

"Please. How do I get free of Cormac? For my son."

"You never get free of that guy," the leader says as he storms away with the rest of the squad following close behind him.

Cloris helps Remo to his feet. She wipes the blood off her SOG blade with his sleeve. That hope Remo was feeling has emptied. Spilled out into the bloody dirt. His face is void. As if he were a robot that had simply been turned off. Cloris looks into his eyes. She waves her hand back and forth in front of them.

Nothing.

She tries again, using both hands.

Nothing.

She slaps him as hard as she can.

Non-responsive.

She runs her tongue over her teeth and says, "Not the time for this shit, man." She points toward the gate as the kill squad charges hard toward it. "We need to fucking engage. Like now."

Remo's eyes drill a hole into a space in the universe that only he can see.

Cloris picks up a Glock off a dead body and jams it into Remo's hand. She cuts his zip tie cuffs free. Remo lets the gun slip and fall from his fingers.

"Suit yourself," Cloris says as she steps away, "but I promise the one sure way to never see your son again is for you to die."

The gunfire outside the walls rages on.

Cloris's words hang in the air. Remo can almost see them typed out in front of him, as if they were in a cartoon comic book bubble pointing from her lips. He knows she's right.

He digs deep. Real deep. Pushing all his self-pity aside, and there's a lot, he starts to move. He'll get back to it later, he's sure.

"Wait," Remo says, moving towards the Glock. "Need a little something."

Cloris grins.

An engine roars.

Remo stands straight up.

Their heads whip toward the sound coming from the east side of the compound. The kill squad leader holds up his fist and turns, facing the east side along with the rest of his team. The roaring engine has their undivided attention.

Cloris grabs Remo by the arm as his fingers fumble and miss picking up the Glock off the ground. Pulling Remo along, they round the corner of the compound where they can see another gate on the east side. A gate that's open. One they didn't realize was there before. One that connects to a driveway. A driveway that is filling with large SUVs—four of them to be exact—and one of them is tearing ass their way.

"Fucking told you there was another way here," Remo says, "*La La, there's no other way*."

"Shut your hole." Cloris says.

The SUV screams toward them at ramming speed.

CHAPTER TWENTY-THREE

LESTER AND HOLLIS wage war like the lords of murder and mayhem they are.

Their weapons blaze. Breathe fire. Puke bullets. They blast in spits and starts then release steady, seamless streams of lead. A sporadic, unpredictable rhythm with no end in sight.

They give 'em some hell.

They get some more in return.

Daddy Mashburn's crew isn't backing down. Not by a damn sight. They return fire. Pounding guns explode into the trees without a clear target in mind. To them it's about creating an uncomfortable place to hide. They know that time is on their side. If they keep up the relentless pressure, whoever's out there will eventually wilt or get dead.

However, these time-honored strategies are not currently working.

Whoever is out in the woods today is more skilled than what Daddy Mashburn's crew is used to.

More dangerous.

Mashburn tells his people to follow their guns.

They'll spot the flash of an AR barrel. They'll see it then shift their blasts to another tree like tracking a traveling firefly. Then a Glock will pop from another. Then another and another. It's as if Daddy Mashburn's crew were fighting a hundred of them.

"It's insane," one of them tells Daddy Mashburn.

Daddy Mashburn is no stranger to a gunfight, but this feels different. He's not seen one like this. A man next to him takes a slug to the shoulder, spins, then grits his teeth and keeps on it. Then another man takes a pop to the forehead. He gets spun, but doesn't keep on it. At all. No. His eyes go blank and his body flies back as if the ghost of Bruce Lee clicked him in the forehead. Daddy Mashburn can see this fight is wearing down his boys. Only a matter of time before the bodies start piling up.

Hollis and Lester keep one thing constant.

Constant movement in one direction.

CHAPTER TWENTY-FOUR

THEY KEEP the pressure up with the blasting, pounding guns, continuing to get closer to the compound. Fighting for every step. Earning every step. Killing for a foot. Spilling blood while gaining ground inch by inch. When this started there were five of them out there, counting Daddy Mashburn. Hollis knows he put one of them down with a headshot. He saw the red plume behind the head and the body flop to the dirt.

Lester knows he put a bullet in one, but he's fairly sure it was only a shoulder. He feels his rage building. Simmering to the top. That thing. That little gift from God that makes him shift from green to red. From the calm, thoughtful man of the Lord to someone—sorry, scratch that, some *thing*—that wouldn't think twice about cutting off a man's head. Type of man who would smash another man's head into the streets of New York over and over again. His focus has reached second-level type stuff. His breathing is deep. Slow. Sucking in and out between gnashed teeth. He's already decided what he's going to do if he is blessed enough to get his hands on one of these motherfuckers, and God fucking help them if they lay a finger on Remo or...

Cloris.

What? Lester thinks. Did her name just slip in there? It did. Lester's head caves in. A mental collapse he wasn't counting on. Not at all. In the heat of battle, did his prehistoric mind just pull up Cloris on his list of people to save? People to protect? Not that she needs protection. She's a badass. It's more like she needs protection from herself. Nonetheless, what the fuck is her name doing popping up in his head like that?

Out of the corner of his eye, Hollis sees his war-buddy has lowered his gun. Lester's eyes are drifting. Far-off gaze taking hold.

"What the fuck, man?" Hollis says. "Get in the game."

It's as if the world has turned into a silent, slow-motion movie for Lester. He sees everything, but it's slowed down to a crawl and someone hit the mute button on the remote. A tree will explode and the bark will separate into the air, splitting into splinters of fragments before his very eyes. He can almost see the bullets in mid-air.

Is his feeling for this woman short-circuiting his brain?

Is this what a breakdown feels like?

The timing is piss-poor, but Lester is accepting it.

"Oh, Lord," Lester says, looking toward the sky, "help me."

Hollis is not in the acceptance phase of things. He grabs Lester by the vest and shakes him hard, slamming his body against the tree. Screams into his face, but Lester can't hear him. His senses still dulled by his mental vacation from the situation. Hollis's lips move but Lester can't make out what he's saying. Hollis keeps screaming the same thing over and over again. The words are coming in a little bit better each time Hollis screams it.

Slowly Lester hears an *R*.

Hollis is encouraged by an ever-so-slight sign of recognition from Lester. He keeps up the screaming as the bullets whiz by. He knows this little pause has cost them a shit-ton of momentum.

Emo comes through to Lester's ears. He perks up. He's coming back online.

Again Hollis screams.

"Remo will die."

Lester's eyes go wide.

"Remo will die if we don't stop them," Hollis screams one last time.

Lester tosses Hollis aside and puts multiple bullets into the face of a man charging around a tree.

Hollis can't help but smile.

CHAPTER TWENTY-FIVE

THE TAHOE MOWS down the CIA kill squad.

Two go airborne. Shoot straight up on impact, bounce over the top of the roaring machine and stick a broken-ankle landing on the other side in a heap of bone and flesh.

Another one is stuck to the grill. Planted like a meaty hood ornament.

The leader dropped to the ground at the last second, thinking there was a chance he could slide under as the Tahoe passed. Instead he caught a bumper to his temple and is currently caught on the rear axle being dragged like a large, muscular rag doll.

The Tahoe skids to a stop. Dirt swirls and plumes. The passenger door flings open. Out steps a Hispanic mountain of a man. Tall as a tower. His muscles have muscles. He grips a 9 mm in his meaty paw. The CIA man on the hood twitches.

The Hispanic mountain puts a bullet in his skull.

Twitching ends.

He turns to Cloris and Remo, studying them. He's not shooting or rushing toward them. He's assessing. Remo and Cloris have no idea what to make of this. Their CIA lifeline just got run over and these people don't seem to be on the same page as the folks waging war outside the gates with Hollis and Lester.

Cloris's face scrunches as she fights to process. She doesn't recognize this guy, or the Tahoes. Sure, she's been away awhile, but not that long. Not to mention, Daddy Mashburn has always been a bit of racist, and would never consider working with Mexicans.

Remo decides "defiant prick" is the way to go with this. It's his steady state, his go-to move, and a strategy that has gotten him this far in life. So, logic suggests one should dance with who brought you here.

"Excuse me, fuck-o," Remo calls out. "Those guys were with us."

Cloris grabs his arm, shaking her head *NO* violently. *Something's not right with this shit here.*

Remo shrugs her off. He's been here before. He's got this.

"You?" the Hispanic Mountain asks, still eyeballing the fuck out of them. "You Remo?"

"I am." Remo nods. "Who the in the good fuck might you be?"

The Hispanic Mountain whistles.

All the Tahoe doors open and four more mountains from Mexico pour out. All big as shit. All just as mean. All armed with guns. Except one. There's one mountain now moving directly toward Remo and Cloris. He has a large axe in one hand and chains wrapped around his other thick fist.

Cloris readies her gun.

Remo squints. *This is new.*

The original Hispanic Mountain gives a hand sign to the other two Tahoes sitting in the driveway on the east side of the compound. One Tahoe's engine fires up and it begins heading toward them, while the other stays, taking a position blocking the back gate.

Remo and Cloris take a step back.

"What's up, Pedro?" Remo says, swallowing hard. Eyes fixed on the axe and chains. "Take a wrong turn at Albuquerque?"

"We were handed simple instructions," Axe and Chains says. "Find Remo and make it hurt."

CHAPTER TWENTY-SIX

HOLLIS SLIPS AROUND A TREE.

This guy didn't even see his death coming, Hollis thinks, right before he fires a blast into the back of the guy's head. As the body falls away, Hollis can see across from him that Lester is holding another by the hair, bashing his head into a tree.

Hollis does the math.

Multiple dead. One wounded. One Daddy Mashburn left.

They are only about fifteen, twenty yards away from the front gate of the compound. The firing has stopped. The woods are actually quiet now. Hollis had been so busy unleashing nasty moves he hadn't noticed the silence.

"What the hell?" Hollis says to himself.

He turns and finds Lester is now stomping his boot heel into the face of another one of Mashburn's crew.

New math.

Only Daddy Mashburn is left.

Hollis hasn't seen him since this fight started. He's kinda hard to miss, too. Big, bald dude running around in the woods sort of sticks out among the foliage, and also doesn't move all that quiet among the brush.

The sound of an engine roars beyond the gate.

Dull thumps of metal colliding with something.

Hollis counts four.

Still no gunshots.

Lester moves over next to Hollis. He wipes some blood from his forehead, picks a clump of something from his sleeve then points up ahead.

Daddy Mashburn is standing in front of the gate, but he's not paying attention to them. He has his back turned to them. Turning back to Hollis and Lester, he makes eye contact and raises his empty hands. A show of good faith. He's not looking to fight, at least not now. Hollis doesn't trust it. Lester certainly doesn't trust it, given the history he has with this man. They both level their guns on him as they move forward. Daddy Mashburn points inside the gates, signals for them to be quiet, and then motions for them to join him, all with his hands open and empty.

A single gunshot rings out beyond the wall.

Hollis and Lester move up quickly with guns on Daddy Mashburn. Hollis makes quick scans left, right and up. Trusts nothing, ever, and won't ever trust a Mashburn, but at the moment he really is out of trustworthy options.

They reach Daddy Mashburn. Hollis places the barrel of his gun on his neck. If he so much as looks at them the wrong way Hollis is going to spray him all over that gate.

Daddy Mashburn simply points through a crack in the gate.

Before Hollis and Lester can even steal a look they hear Remo say, "Excuse me, fuck-o..."

CHAPTER TWENTY-SEVEN

AXE AND CHAINS stalks toward Cloris and Remo.

He actually moves past Cloris, heading straight toward Remo.

"We got no beef with you. Only want that one," the lead Hispanic Mountain says to her.

She holds her gun on Axe and Chains as he passes, then rotates her aim to the rest of the Hispanic mountains, attempting to hold them at bay.

"That one you can have," Cloris says.

Remo holds his arms out. *What the fuck?*

He backs up as Axe and Chains gets closer and closer. Remo looks behind him. He's being moved, backed up toward the wall. Seconds away from being backed into it and completely trapped. Axe and Chains lets the chains clink and drop down to the ground, still holding the end with his thick-ass fist. Remo does the only thing an honorable man can do at a moment like this.

He kicks him in the balls.

It does nothing.

Remo kicks his junk again, then again, harder, but still nothing.

The axe rises.

Remo thinks of that Glock Cloris handed him.

The one he dropped. The one over there. He hates how stupid he is sometimes.

The chains come at him. A hard swing clinking, cutting through the air whips toward Remo's head. He ducks. If he moved a hair less the chains would have taken his head clean off.

The axe chops down. Remo dives.

It thunks into the ground an inch from where he was standing. Would have cut him clean in half. Axe and Chains resets, pulling the axe from the ground and cocking back his chains. He stands over Remo.

Remo lies frozen. Fear has removed his ability to do anything. He doesn't scream, fight or even consider being an asshole. This is Remo shutting down.

This is Remo understanding this is game over.

Three shots rip up the back of Axe and Chains.

The pops start between his shoulder blades, working up to the back of his head. He falls face-first into the wall with his forehead sliding down from the lubrication provided from the exit wound.

Remo twists away, jumping to his feet.

Game back on.

It's as if his brain had taken a break for a moment. A defense mechanism he supposes, but he's back. Just needed a second. A new battle is raging in front of him. He must have blocked this all out as well while he was accepting his own death.

He sees the bodies.

The blood.

The muzzle flashes are fast as Hollis and Daddy Mashburn blast away at a Tahoe that's speeding toward them. Holes carve up the hood and pop the windshield as it rambles closer and closer.

All Remo can think is, *When did they all become buddy-buddy?*

Remo then sees Lester on top of the Hispanic Mountain. His knees pinning him down as Lester pounds away at his skull with the butt of his AR.

Remo sees Cloris too. She's unloading her Glock at the speeding Tahoe, taking a position next to her daddy with Hollis on the other side. She slams in a fresh seventeen rounds.

What the fuck did I miss? thinks Remo.

His mind clicks as he watches the mayhem unfold in front of him. Cloris. The woman who only seconds ago let Axe and Chains pass her by and said something about "fuck Remo." He's paraphrasing, but that's pretty much how it went down. He didn't miss that shit.

Remo picks up the axe and moves toward them. He limps and drags himself forward. Must have fucked up his leg somewhere in all this mess. Hard to pinpoint when exactly, but he's got a limp to be sure.

The remaining friends of Hispanic Mountain by the back gate have engaged, joining the fight as well. They open fire from across the compound.

Remo feels himself slipping away. He's never come to this place in his mind before. Maybe this is how Lester feels sometimes. This redline of rage. Remo gets it now. He feels completely okay with cutting off someone's head at the moment. It's a comforting idea, if Remo's honest. The idea of killing Cloris is very comforting.

The battle at the Hamptons didn't trigger this.

The Russian roulette at Crow's place didn't bring him to this point in his life.

No, this desire is purely vengeance-based, and it's a new one for Remo.

He drags the axe behind him like a deranged serial killer, limping slowly toward her. He leans down and picks up the Glock on the ground, tucking it behind his back. He might use that later, but not now.

No.

She gets the axe.

Remo doesn't know what her game is, but he knows for damn certain it doesn't involve Remo living happily ever after.

The Tahoe swerves. A bullet-riddled body spills and falls from the driver's side, rolling in the dirt. The driverless Tahoe cuts harder now with no one at the wheel. The large SUV cuts hard toward the wall, slamming into the metal then bouncing backward a foot and a half.

Remo is getting closer.

Closer to Cloris.

She's completely unaware, as she keeps alternating her blasts between the recently-crashed Tahoe and the other crew parked by the east gate. She has no idea what's headed toward her. Unaware that Remo and his axe are coming for her.

A man flings open a rear door of the crashed Tahoe. He slides out, only to be cut up like Sonny C in *Part I*. Once he flops, Hollis, Daddy Mashburn and Cloris turn their attention fully on the group down by the east gate. Hollis uses controlled bursts, whereas Daddy Mashburn and Cloris scream and wail, firing at will without control or thought.

Remo pushes forward step by step.

The gunfire booms.

He's a few feet away from Cloris.

He raises the axe above his head.

"Remo!" Lester calls out. "Don't."

Remo tilts his attention to him.

A large foot slams into Remo's gut, sending him flying backward with the axe still in hand. Daddy Mashburn just kicked the shit out of him, almost literally, and is storming his way. Protecting his daughter with a vengeance. Nobody raises an axe to his little girl, and certainly not the fucking lawyer who killed his sons. Daddy Mashburn's sight has blurred to white as the rage has taken hold of him. He charges toward Remo with the speed and force of a man on fire.

Remo tries to use the axe handle to help himself up, but slips and falls back to the ground. The axe slips from his grip.

Daddy Mashburn shoves it away with one foot and in a single motion stomps his other foot down on Remo's chest. The pain is sharp. Immediate. All air leaves Remo's body. Daddy Mashburn's foot lifts up and slams down again and again and again.

Vision is leaving Remo. Leaving fast. The world blurs.

Daddy Mashburn picks Remo up by the collar, holding him up off the ground. He wants Remo to see what's coming.

"You killed my sons," he barks through grinding teeth.

Remo feels around behind his back for the Glock. It's not there. His fingers fumble, panic-searching for something that's simply not there. Out of the corner of his eye he sees the gun on the ground next to him. *Fuuuuuck.*

Remo knows he's left with the only weapon he has available. His constant, never-ending arsenal. His weapon of choice.

Being a complete asshole.

"I did," Remo says. "Had some help, but yes, I did kill them and guess what, big boy? I. Fucking. Liked. It."

Daddy Mashburn head-butts him. Remo's nose splits just shy of exploding. After the beatings he's taken today, one would think there wouldn't be any blood left in his face, but oh yes, there is. Blood pours down his mouth and chin. Remo fights passing out, pulling out a smile.

"Your sons died like a pack of cunts. Ya know that, Daddy-O? They cried and bitched and bitched and cried. Oh, and the begging. Holy fucking shit the begging. You would have been sooooo embarrassed."

Something breaks behind Daddy Mashburn's eyes. Snaps. He has wanted to find this man, this Remo Cobb, ever since he heard what he did to his boys. What he did to his family. And now he has him in his hands and he is going to fuck this boy up something ferocious.

Remo closes his eyes in anticipation of what is about to come his way.

He feels his body fall. The drop. The weightlessness. He feels the impact with the ground. Fucking hurts, but he's alive. He cracks one eye open.

Standing above him is a headless Daddy Mashburn.

His massive body is there, but his head is gone.

His neck stump spits blood out in short then longer bursts, firing up into the air like a busted sprinkler. After a second or two his body falls away revealing Cloris holding the axe with both hands. Her body is fully twisted around as if she just took a major-league swing.

Remo sees Daddy Mashburn's head roll past his Glock.

Lester steps next to her, places a hand on her shoulder and carefully removes the axe from her fingers. She's shaken. Her breathing is erratic. Her face drained of color, turning her white as a sheet.

"What the fuck is wrong with you people?" Remo yells. "With the heads and the cutting and the chopping of heads?" He gets up, holding his gushing nose. "Seriously, what the fuck?"

Remo notices the gunfire has stopped. With a quick glance he sees the eastside gate is littered with several motionless bodies, along with a Tahoe pocked to hell with gashes and holes.

Cloris looks up to Lester.

She wraps her fingers in his. He lets her.

She's searching for something. Hunting for an answer that's locked inside his head. One that only he can open up and share with her. He looks down to her. His face is unreadable. A typical expression for Lester. Always seconds away from spirituality or brutality. The switch flips both ways, but it is hard to know which way until it goes.

Hollis moves to them with his AR on Cloris. He saw what she did with Remo. How she let Axe and Chains move past her toward him, and what she said. Hollis is the one who ripped three shots into Axe and Chains. He also saw what she did to Daddy Mashburn. That one has Remo and Hollis both puzzled as shit. Her actions don't match clear motives.

The thought occurs to Remo that she doesn't have any.

Chaos motivates her. She simply operates from minute to minute and her reasons sixty seconds ago may or may not apply to the current sixty seconds.

This scares the shit out of Remo.

Hollis too, which is why he has his AR leveled on her at the moment.

Lester glances to Hollis. "Put it down."

"She almost got Remo killed," Hollis says. "She was going to let it happen, man. You and I both saw the whole damn thing."

"It's true. She fucking did, man," Remo says.

Lester's eyes bounce between the three of them. To Hollis, to Cloris, then to Remo. Remo. His reason for being here. The reason he came back. The one asshole who needed saving. His eyes slip back over to Cloris. He has loved the woman, and probably still does. He looks at her as if trying to read her soul. As if he could.

She tries to explain herself without saying a word. Tries to let her eyes, her lips, her face tell him everything he needs to know. That she is still the woman he loves and needs. It's still just Cloris, despite all the crazy, and they can be together and be happy as hell. It's a lot get out with just a look, so she decides to throw some words onto the fire.

"I knew he wouldn't do it," she says. "I knew the axe and chain guy wouldn't do it."

"How in the fuck did you know that?" Remo says.

"It was soooo obvious," she says, leaving that impenetrable argument to stand. She lets silence wash over the conversation, hoping everyone will move on.

Remo is not moving on.

"Well, that clears everything up," Remo says. "Can't even begin to argue with that. Don't worry about it. We're cool."

"She *did* kill Daddy Mashburn," Lester adds. "Right before he was going to kill you."

"I know, right?" Remo says. "It's a real head-scratcher with her. I do not get what the hell is going on with this one." He turns and asks, "Hollis? Thoughts?"

"I don't trust anything about her. She's completely out of control." Hollis re-grips his AR. "She can make some damn fine chicken, but shit, she's a whacko."

Cloris's veins pop.

Hollis smiles big. Blows her a kiss. He's testing her.

She becomes unhinged inside. She's failing the test.

Cloris jumps at Hollis. It's all Lester can do to hold her back. Like a rabid beast going after fresh meat.

"See?" Hollis says. "See that shit?"

"Stop," Lester says.

"You know it's true," Hollis says. "She would kill us all and you fucking know it, man."

Lester's expression hardens. Hollis sees what's happening. So does Remo and he hates it.

"I know you care about her," Hollis says to Lester, "but she's no good, man. We can't count on anything about her."

"Stop," Lester says again.

"We just watched her cut her father's head off, for fuck's sake," Hollis insists.

Lester struggles holding her back. He's losing his grip. She's reached a new, higher level of pissed off. She's lost the ability to form a complete word in English, let alone a sentence. She's barking, hissing in a jumbled form of rage-speak. Eyes bulging. Face fire-engine red.

"I know," Lester says, fighting to hold on. "I know what you're saying—"

She breaks loose from Lester, tearing ass toward Hollis. Hollis fires a single shot. Tags her in the shoulder. It barely slows her down. She springs from her feet, launching into Hollis like she was shot from a cannon. They tumble to the ground much like they did back at the house.

Spit flies.

Fists. Elbows. Palms of hands.

Hollis lands a punch.

Cloris bites his neck then chomps on his ear.

Lester dives into the fray. His arms tugging at the sporadic movements of angry people bent on murder. Hands fumbling and slipping away as he tries to pull them apart, but he can't. They are both strong as hell and burning on high-octane, rage-fueled hate.

A gun goes off. Lester feels the air zip by his face. He has no idea who triggered the shot, since they both have guns raised. Both of them fighting to angle a kill shot on the other. Lester goes from green to red. Flips to instinct rather than thought. He plows headfirst into the tumbling mass of violent humanity.

Remo can only stand on the sidelines, holding his bleeding nose.

He picks up the Glock, tucking it under his shirt. Just in case.

He watches as his *team* dissolves in front of him. Even in the middle of this chaos in the mountains, he feels the twinge of failure. Failed leadership. Remo feels he was a good leader, at least he tried, but his rule was set up to fail, considering the players he was given. No matter if this is the truth or not, it does comfort Remo. It's not really his fault. Not entirely. The coach always takes the blame.

It happens.

Remo is solid as a leader.

He's snapped free from his thoughts when the cold barrel of a gun presses hard against his temple. A hand grabs his shoulder tightly.

"We gotta bounce, Remo," Cormac says.

CHAPTER TWENTY-EIGHT

REMO SEES CORMAC.

Can't believe it.

Not sure what it means, but Cormac is sure as shit here and standing next to him with a gun pressed to his head. Cormac pulls at him. Tugs his arm hard with the gun still planted, digging into his temple. Cormac is manhandling Remo away toward the east gate.

Away from his companions.

Away from his team.

Away from his friends. Well, Cloris is hard to put in the "friend" bucket, but she's what passes for friendship these days. At least for Remo.

Remo doesn't even bother fighting it. *What's the point?* Something has shut down inside of him. As if the *We're Open* sign on his front window has been turned around and now reads *Fucking Done*. Resignation is taking hold, and Remo may even like it.

As he's moved away he watches them fight. They are really going at it. Cloris, Lester and Hollis locked in battle. Remo can't help but try to place odds on the thing. Logic suggests Hollis, given his training and experience, will take this thing in the end, but Lester could easily come out on top with his maniac switch flipped on. And Cloris? Shit, Cloris could kill them both and then go have pizza and watch a movie and not think twice about the whole thing.

Remo's mind wanders further.

Fumbling.

Tumbling.

Farther and farther down a dark twirl of memories tangled with emotional knots he'd rather not unspool. The losses he's piled up recently. The loss of it all. He never dealt with the loss of his New York life. His job. His status. Certainly didn't get to deal with the upside of meeting his son, which made up for all the other losses. For a fraction of a sliver of a moment in time Remo understood that *happy* thing people talk about so much. At least he felt it once before he bit the big one. That much he can be thankful for.

He can almost feel himself peeling away from the here and now.

His mind lifting up, not accepting what's happening.

He thinks of his dream about Sean in the woods and Anna taking him away. Then the angry, headless hordes coming at him. He shook awake before they got to him, as you do in dreams but don't get to in real life.

You wake up from falling right before you make impact.

Before the monster rips you apart.

Something inside you jolts awake during the ones that scare the shit out of you. Then you sit up in bed wondering what the hell that was all about.

Now that he's wide awake, living in this meat grinder of a life, he lets that dream play out in his broken mind as he's leaving his friends behind. He goes back to those woods at night. Next to the campfire watching his son and ex-wife move away from him. He sees the headless hordes rambling toward him with their crude weapons made of bone. He imagines they get hold of him, tearing away at his flesh with their bare hands. Yanking it all clean from the bones. Hacking away at him. He imagines himself screaming in terror. Face twisted in indescribable pain.

No.

Scratch that.

He imagines himself standing there with a blank expression plastered on his face. Serene. Eyes glazed over with zero sign of emotion or thought. Mouth closed with an ever so slight smirk planted on his lips.

A look of complete understanding regarding his position in life.

Pure acceptance.

Acceptance that world had finally eaten him alive.

CHAPTER TWENTY-NINE

A FIRM HAND slaps the shit out of Remo's face.

Cormac's hand.

Remo snaps to.

He'd let his head drift a bit. Checked out of the here and now, perhaps letting denial take him by the hand and lead him to a place where this disaster he's in isn't truly his life. A dream that this isn't the world he's living in. Where he's not riding in a beaten-down Chevy truck that CIA dickhole Cormac explained earlier that he stole. They are roaring at an unsafe speed through the narrow, winding mountain roads of New Mexico. Remo peeks over the side of the road. They are way the hell up and it's a steep dive down the side of the mountain.

The last he saw Hollis, Cloris and Lester they were engaged in a vicious display of hand-to-hand combat at the Mashburn compound. Dead bodies were scattered about the place, including a headless Daddy Mashburn. Remo thinks he's come a long way only to get back where he started from—another home littered with the dead, another headless Mashburn.

The more things change, the more they stay the same.

There are a couple of new wrinkles this time. One in particular strikes Remo at the moment.

There's a car following them.

Cormac hasn't said it, but Remo can tell. Cormac is nervous. Twitchy. Not the cold, in control, calm Lord of the CIA Remo has come to know and hate. This Cormac speaks in spits and starts. Can't form a clear, complete sentence. He clutches his gun in a shaky hand, turning around constantly checking on the car that's on them.

Cormac told Remo earlier that they had to leave the compound. Sorry, he said they needed to *bounce*. Told Remo at gunpoint to be exact, then led Remo to this truck. A rusted, used-to-be-red Chevy that still runs like a mad beast of a V8 machine. Cormac fights to control the car. Driving like a crazy person. Hands gripping the wheel so tight his knuckles pop then fade to white. Doing everything he can to take the truck on turns well beyond the recommended speed limit. Cormac and Remo sway and bounce around inside the truck's cab like dice thrown on a craps table.

"Get off me, motherfucker," Cormac says to the rearview mirror.

"Perhaps he doesn't like you," Remo says, digging his fingertips into the dashboard for dear life.

"Perhaps, but I know he doesn't like you," Cormac says.

"Doesn't rule a lot of people out."

"Look, I screwed this up. I know I did, but it is what it is and we're going to work through it all."

"You're going to need to clarify."

"Well." Cormac takes a moment, looks back, looks to Remo and then spills it. "I might have let it leak what you did with the Mashburn case."

Remo blinks.

"You know, " Cormac explains, "that you stole the Mashburns' money and framed them and then killed them."

"When you say *might have* and *leaked...*"

"Let's say a lot. Leaked to everybody, actually. All your clients, I mean. And your former clients did not respond well to this news. A few of the larger ones have brought in some hired hands to remove you."

Remo's mind slides in and out of place. That's what was up with the Hispanic Mountain and friends. They were with the Diaz brothers. He thought he recognized the one, but it was hard to place him through the fog of fear. They had nothing to do with Daddy Mashburn and everything to do with Remo. Remo can think of several past clients who might call in a hard-hitting crew like that if they thought Remo was doing them wrong. If Cormac somehow confirmed that Remo fucked over the Mashburns then, well, that would definitely trigger some calls.

But that's only one.

There are dozens who could, would and probably *did* make some calls.

"When I say they hired hands to *remove you*, you know I mean *kill you*, right?"

"I get it," Remo says. "Is that who's behind us?"

Cormac nods, checking his mirrors again.

Remo should be more concerned than he is. He's uncomfortable with how well he's taking this. Uncomfortable with how comfortable he's becoming with folks trying to kill him. Maybe he's simply getting used to constantly being the target of killers and thieves. He's not proud of it, but it's where his head is. His big brain keeps flipping through the hows and whys of the situation in an attempt to construct a way out. He keeps fumbling around one question as they continue to slip and slide along the truck's bench seat. A question that has been eating at him ever since Cormac came into his life.

"Why the CIA?" Remo asks. "Why were you so damned interested in me and my clients to begin with? International gunrunning? Global money laundering schemes? What? What was it?"

Cormac looks to Remo then back to the road. There's an almost-shame wave that spreads over his face. He starts to speak, stops, tries again, thinks, and then says, "It's not what you think."

"Okay. Explain. Talk to me like I was five," Remo says.

"There was a bartender you used to date not long ago," Cormac says. "She left you, said you were an asshole and you didn't respect her."

Remo hangs on to the dashboard again as they almost slide off the road and over into the abyss. He regroups and thinks. He tries to think of a woman who meets that description. It's difficult, given the number of candidates. More than a few who consider him an asshole.

Then one comes to mind.

He thinks of the woman he faked an orgasm with. The one who worked at the hipster bar. The one he bought the boob job for a while back. He remembers respect wasn't really held on either side, but lets that part go.

"Okay..." Remo says.

"Well, she's my sister. She came over to my house in tears and wanted me to do something to you. Wanted me to dig into your life and find something to squeeze. I checked you out and found out there was probably some tax stuff I could hand to the IRS, but then you did the Mashburn thing in the Hamptons and I realized I could use you to take care of some other stuff."

"Wait. Let me get this straight," Remo says, rubbing his temples. "I pissed off your sister and you figured out a way to use the shit out of me?"

"Started that way. Then I kept digging and digging and the layers kept piling on. There was Hollis and Lester and then Cloris and it all fell into place. I could create a great little task force of convenience that I could leverage."

"When was it going to end?" Remo asks.

Cormac checks behind him, ignoring the question. They've reached the bottom of the mountain and are moving through a small town. Remo looks back and sees there are now two cars on them.

Remo remembers the Glock. He makes a quick feel in the front of his pants. It's still there. In the middle of all the craziness, Cormac didn't pat him down.

"There's a safe house up here," Cormac says. "We can stop there. I can talk to these guys behind us."

"When, fucker?" Remo barks. "When was all this going to end? What was your plan?"

"There wasn't a specific finish date." Cormac swallows hard. "It was over when you were dead or no longer of use to me."

Remo looks out the window, watching the brown and tan of the New Mexico town pass by. He feels foolish. Stupid for thinking he had a chance to be with his son. He let the illusion of hope cloud what he knew about life. The knowledge that we're all fucked no matter what we do. He can feel himself dissolve inside, letting all the hope that had built up inside of him drain out into the floorboard of this piece of shit truck.

He presses pause on his pity party for one.

One simple truth clicks as they make a turn, leaving the town and moving out toward wide-open nothingness. There's a single home on a plot of land in the distance. Remo knows that must be where they are headed. Out of the way. Somewhat secluded. The simple truth Remo unearthed is now confirmed.

"The people coming after me now," Remo says, "they got to you first, didn't they? Me, Hollis, Lester and Cloris, we're an off-the-books operation. The rest of the CIA, or any law enforcement for that matter, they don't know anything about us. Aside from Detective Harris, the way you got to me. And he's dirty as fuck, so he's not going to say shit, right?"

Cormac stares at the road and the house up ahead as they drive closer and closer. Remo glances to the rearview. Now three cars are on them and not another soul on the road.

"They got to you. Threatened you with God-knows-what and

now you're serving me up on a platter to save your own bitch ass," Remo says. "You can't call in the rest of the CIA, because then they'll know you went off the reservation, all because I pissed off your sister. I bought her tits, for fuck's sake."

Cormac drives off the main road onto the dirt path leading up to the house. He glances back. The three cars are following.

"Tell me I'm wrong," Remo presses. "Lie to me. At least give me that."

"You're right," Cormac finally admits. "I had a few people I called on, the kill squad back there and whatnot, but yeah, overall it's a damn mess."

Cormac jams it in park.

Remo looks back. The three cars will be there in seconds. Cormac clucks his tongue and reaches for his gun. Remo pulls his Glock from under his shirt. Cormac fires a shot as Remo lunges forward slamming into the dash. The back window explodes. Remo twists, firing three blasts. The first blows out the driver's window behind Cormac. The second and third tear apart Cormac's neck and face. His body slumps over, lying on the horn.

The cars are only a few feet from turning into the driveway.

The horn blares.

Remo grabs the keys and pushes Cormac off the horn. He grabs Cormac's gun. He needs all he can get.

Flying from the truck, he stumble-runs to the back of the house, charging hard to the back door as the three cars skid to a stop in the gravel driveway behind the truck.

The back door of the house opens as Remo gets within a foot of it. Another CIA man steps out, armed with an assault rifle.

"Where's Cormac?" the CIA man asks, raising his AR.

Thank God, Remo thinks as he fires a shot, dropping the CIA man. Remo knows he'll need that assault rifle and whatever else he can get off this asshole.

The cars start to unload a mishmash of bad dudes. There's no color coding of race with this crew. No uniforms or matching tats.

Simply a pack of mean dudes from every walk of life with guns in hand and murder in their hearts. They explode out from the car doors, ready to rock.

Remo scampers into the house, slamming the door behind him.

He locks it for some reason.

He checks the windows. The bad dudes are surrounding the house. They take positions at every possible angle. He can hear boots and shoes thump and patter down the sides. Remo's been in this situation before. Trapped in a house, pinned down by heavily armed, evil dildos wishing do him harm. Only last time it was in his own home in the Hamptons.

Last time there were fewer bad guys who wanted Remo dead.

Last time he had more guns.

Last time he was a bit of a pussy.

Times have changed.

Remo puts one in the chamber.

CHAPTER THIRTY

REMO CHECKS THE WINDOW.

More of a formality than anything. He knew what he'd see out there, but just needed to see it with his own eyes. They haven't started shooting or busting down the door. At least not yet. That's a good sign.

Maybe.

They have all their guns pointed at the house, scanning the windows and the doors, but they haven't opened up on him. At least not yet. They're waiting for something. *But what?* They know damn well Remo is in here alone. So why not finish this thing? Remo sees another man step out from the last car.

Remo realizes why, now.

A tall, slender man with hair cut close to the skull moves toward the house. He nods as one of the bad dude dildos tells him something. The slender man slides on some shades and moves with the swagger of a man without a care in the world and a dick the size of King Kong. He's dressed in a casual, cool style that cost him thousands. Remo is a little annoyed with the fact that even at a time like this he can calculate the cost of this guy's outfit. Holdover from his former life. *Can't help it,* he tells himself.

Remo knows this guy.

Hates this guy.

Used to have this guy as a client.

Justin Slim. J. Slim they call him. He is a man similar to Hollis. A contract killer, but with only one client, and that client is what has Remo moments away from pissing his pants.

"Remo," J. Slim calls out.

Remo says nothing, checks the AR.

"Remo, I know you can hear me. So I'll keep talking even if you don't return the favor."

J. Slim pauses on the off chance Remo will give up his position and he can go grab a drink and screw a local.

"Ray's not happy, as you can probably guess. Sure you've got a few former clients who feel the same," J. Slim says. "You fucked up, Remo. You really did. I don't know if you did us like you did the Mashburns..."

Remo opens the door a crack and bounces back, hoping he's not cut down by a storm of lead. When the bullets don't fly, he leans by the edge of the door and calls out, "I didn't do shit to Ray or you, motherfucker."

J. Slim cracks a smile. *Ahhh, Remo.* "Yeah, but the problem now is, how can we trust you? I mean every little thing that's gone wrong they can now pin directly on you, right or wrong. You see?"

Remo shuts his eyes tight. *Shit.* Cormac has made Remo the perfect scapegoat for every criminal organization on the planet.

How did the cops find us? Remo.

How did that get so fucked up? Remo.

Who took our fucking money? Remo.

Who did the thing about the thing? Remo.

"What do you do here, Remo? We're outside town, but not that far. If we start blasting it out with you the cops will eventually come and that doesn't do anybody any good. Think about it. You're hunkered down on a property with two dead CIA agents. That won't play well."

Remo bites his lip.

Thinks of Sean.

Thinks of putting a bullet in J. Slim and starting this thing off. If he can drop J. Slim he can start picking off the rest one by one, then jack one of these cars and get gone before the small-town, law-and-order mutts show up for the party. Remo can't believe this is how mutated his thinking has become. He used to think about suit fabric, good scotch and pussy. Now he's plotting mass murder at a CIA safe house, with an escape plan to boot.

Never stop learning, he thinks.

He takes aim on J. Slim's head. Fingers the trigger.

He can envision J. Slim's head bursting like a melon.

"I don't want a bloodbath here, Remo. I don't," J. Slim says, then motions to one of his bad dude dildos. "I can't see a way this ends with you alive, but I can make it as painless as possible."

The bad dude dildo takes something from J. Slim and moves toward the front of the house. Remo watches him holster his gun and walk to the front door. Remo positions himself behind a couch and takes aim at the front door. He waits for the firestorm to come.

It doesn't.

He hears the boots and footsteps patter as they move away from the house, followed by the sound of car doors closing. Out the window Remo watches the cars back up and leave the driveway. Only dirt in the wind.

Remo moves around the house checking all the windows. Looking to make sure there wasn't some dildo left behind to take Remo out when his guard is down. He gives the place a few good scans but doesn't find anyone.

Remo takes a deep breath and opens the front door wider.

Just a crack more, letting him get a peak of what's outside.

The dirt yard is empty. Only a plant that's barely alive and a three-legged dog hobbling down the gravel road barking at him.

At his feet on the faded *Welcome Home* mat is an iPad with a Post-it note stuck on the screen.

There's a New York street address printed on the Post-it, along with the words, *Tap then meet us here!*

Remo's stomach drops through the ground before he even taps the screen.

With a single touch of his finger a video image of Sean and Anna playing at a park appears in crystal-clear HD. They are playing at a park Remo knows well. The same park Remo stumbled into after his battle in the Hamptons. Sean is laughing and running. Anna is chasing. Remo can't help but want to smile, but a tear rolls instead.

The camera turns around to face the man who's filming them. Remo doesn't recognize the man, but he knows the look. Sharp-dressed criminal. A high-net-worth asshole who's been upped from street murder boy to Manhattan resident based on his body count. Remo also recognizes the look in his eyes.

This guy is a killer.

This man enjoys the pain of others.

This man waves to the camera.

To Remo.

COMING SOON

REMO WENT OFF, the fourth book in the Remo Cobb series, will hit the world late 2017... maybe earlier... perhaps later... who's to say?

ALSO BY MIKE MCCRARY

The Remo Cobb Series

Remo Went Rogue

Remo Went Down

Remo Went Wild

The Steady Teddy Series

Steady Trouble

Steady Madness (Coming Soon)

Standalone Books

Genuinely Dangerous

Getting Ugly

ABOUT THE AUTHOR

I've been a waiter, screenwriter, a securities trader, dishwasher, bartender, investment analyst and an unpaid Hollywood intern. I've quit corporate America, come back, been fired, been promoted, been fired again. Currently, I write stories about questionable people who make questionable decisions.

Always great to hear from you. Please follow or contact me at:

www.mikemccrary.com

mccrarynews@mikemccrary.com

ACKNOWLEDGMENTS

You can't do a damn thing alone, so I'd like to thank the people who gave me help and hope during this little fun and self-loathing writing life.

First, thanks to Elmore Leonard, Don Winslow, Stephen King, Chuck Palahniuk, Duane Swierczynski, Charlie Huston and Dennis Lehane. You don't know me, but thank you for what you do. Thanks, in no particular order, to the following writers, bad-asses, good dudes and Book Gods: Blake Crouch, Tom Pitts, Allan Guthrie, Joe Clifford, John Rector, Peter Farris and Johnny Shaw. Thank you for talking books and the publishing world with me, even if you didn't know you were doing it.

Big, massive, sloppy love to the good folks at MXN Entertainment (Michelle Knudsen and Mason Novick) for never wavering in their help and support over the years, thank you doesn't cover it, man. Michelle, thank you for the greatest note ever, "Why did you kill Lester? He's the best part."

Love and appreciation to my family and friends who have put up with me and my bullshit—you know who are. Thanks to Mom and Dad for not selling me for medical experiments, and last but not least, thank you to my amazing family. You have endured and embraced me during my bitter, cranky, moody and (let's just say it) dark days. For that and for everything, every day. I love you.

Copyright © 2017 by Mike McCrary

Cover by JT Lindros

This is a work of fiction in which all names, characters, places and events are imaginary. Where names of actual celebrities, organizations and corporate entities are used, they're used for fictional purposes and don't constitute actual assertions of fact. No resemblance to anyone or anything real is intended, nor should it be inferred.

No part of this publication may be reproduced, stored in a retrieval system, or transmitted in any form by any means without the written consent of the publisher, with the exception of brief excerpts for the purpose of review or promotion.

5/22

71131448R00099

Made in the USA
Middletown, DE
20 April 2018